"Wait a minute, those are our horses!"

Jessica swung around. The nearer of the two braves reached out and caught a lock of her hair. He barely had time to feel it between his fingers before Ki's fist caught him in the mouth and knocked him from his horse.

Ki leaped from the wagon and crashed headfirst into the other brave. They both tumbled to the ground. Ki sprang to his feet quickly, and turned to face the first brave. The Indian stood opposite him, a long hunting knife drawn and at the ready.

As soon as Jessie realized what was happening, she reached for her revolver. But before her hand could clear her jacket pocket, the Comanche leader had his lance just inches from her neck.

Her fingers let the gun drop . . .

S0-AGF-628

Also in the LONE STAR series
from Jove

WESLEY ELLIS

LONE STAR

AND THE
INDIAN REBELLION

A JOVE BOOK

LONE STAR AND THE INDIAN REBELLION

A Jove Book/published by arrangement with
the author

PRINTING HISTORY
Jove edition/October 1986

All rights reserved.
Copyright © 1986 by Jove Publications, Inc.
This book may not be reproduced in whole or in part,
by mimeograph or any other means, without permission.
For information address: The Berkley Publishing Group,
200 Madison Avenue, New York, N.Y. 10016.

ISBN: 0-515-08716-5

Jove Books are published by the Berkley Publishing Group,
200 Madison Avenue, New York, N.Y. 10016. The words
"A JOVE BOOK" and the "J" with sunburst are trademarks
belonging to Jove Publications, Inc.

PRINTED IN THE UNITED STATES OF AMERICA

To Lone Wolf,
a friend gone but not forgotten,
and
to Rick Martin Nayer

Chapter 1

On the near-frozen ground of the Staked Plains the buck-board left no sign of its passing. No dust clouds and no wheel ruts. But for once, stealth and secrecy were not a concern of the two occupants of the wagon.

Jessie Starbuck sat with the reins lying loosely in her lap, and before she realized it her eyes had closed lazily. Momentarily she remained poised on the brink of sleep, then jerked her head up with a start. Her clear green eyes were instantly alert, and a slow smile crossed her pretty face. The tall, good-looking man who sat beside her noticed her reaction, and smiled too.

"I guess old habits die hard, huh, Ki?"

"Vigilance is not a frivolous trait, Jessie."

"But it seems so unnecessary now." Her eyes took in the expanse of the plateau they now traveled across. For as far as the eye could see there was no change in the land, no landmark, and no sign of man, past or present.

"If you are referring to the death of the cartel, I'd have to agree with you, but if you're talking about the security of all this"—he began to shake his head slowly—"it can be deceiving. A few braves or bushwhackers could hide in one of the larger buffalo wallows, and you'd be on them before you realized it."

Jessie studied Ki. In all the years she had known him he

1

seemed to have changed little. Even though he was just a young man when her father first brought the half-Japanese, half-American to this country to act as her bodyguard, Ki had always been tall, strong, and very masculine. His dark hair had always been shiny and long, and he always wore that same smile. It had taken her years to figure out Ki's sense of humor, and even now she wasn't so sure. His face was always smooth and beardless. The pencil-thin mustache that clung to his upper lip was the exception. Jessie knew he hadn't always had that, but for the life of her she couldn't picture him without it. Ki must have changed some, Jessie realized, but being so close to him day in, day out made it hard to see the change. She had been just a young girl when Ki first came to the Circle Star. Then he had been very much her teacher, but now she was a full-grown woman. She often wondered if Ki ever noticed. "And old roles are hard to change," she commented aloud.

Ki was not thrown by the apparent shift in the conversation. "I see no reason for them to change," he stated flatly. There was a slight pause, and Jessie considered his response. She wondered if he really understood what she had meant. "Cartel or no cartel, I'm still concerned with your safety. I wouldn't let anything happen to you, Jessie."

Jessie started to speak, then stopped herself abruptly. She had been about to say that there had to be more to it than just Ki's sense of duty and obligation. But she realized how pointless an observation that would be. Jessie herself had risked her life many times when she thought Ki was in danger, and of course duty and responsibility had nothing to do with it. "But still, it's nice not to have to always be looking over your shoulder, or as you put it," she added with a smile, "into every buffalo wallow."

"You are still not without enemies." Apparently Ki had more to say on the subject. "Any businesswoman in your position is bound to have a few enemies—"

"Yes, but few of them wish us dead. And even those few are unlikely to try and put a bullet in the back of our heads." Ki seemed unimpressed. "And most importantly, Ki," Jessie added with emphasis, "none have the power of the cartel."

The memory of the syndicate that had caused both her parents' deaths still brought her pain. While she and Ki had battled the cartel, that pain had been channeled into anger and action, but now, with the cartel destroyed and its evil gone, there was no reason to dwell on the subject. She wrapped the long sheepskin jacket a little tighter around her legs. "Do you think we'll make the lowlands by tonight, Ki?"

"I hope so. It may not be any warmer there, but I think the night winds won't blow as fierce." Ki reached behind him and pulled out a wool blanket. He opened it and spread it out across their laps. Ki, like Jessie, was also bundled in a sheepskin jacket, but unlike Jessie's, which was long enough to cover her legs, Ki's jacket was waist-length. He preferred to keep his legs, a powerful weapon in themselves, free and unencumbered.

Jessie moved an inch closer to Ki. "Thank you, Ki. For everything."

The sun had just dipped below the horizon when they reached the adobe-and-sod structure. Since Ki had spotted the thin wisps of smoke curling up from the chimney a few miles back, they had both been looking forward to a hot meal and a warm place to sleep. But now a husky man stood in the doorway and pointed his Winchester directly at them.

Jessie understood the natural tendency for homesteaders always to be on their guard, but something in the man's stance seemed unnecessarily hostile. She noticed he seemed more interested in the wagon than in the two strangers who stood before him. After their earlier discussion it would be ironic for some sodbuster to try and rob them. There wasn't much of a chance that he could succeed, but it would certainly add emphasis to Ki's comments. Jessie groaned to herself over the fact that, once again, Ki would prove to be right. He was never one to say, "I told you so," but even unspoken, it still annoyed her. What rankled her more was the probability they'd be spending another cold night under the stars.

"You folks are a long way from anywhere," the man said suspiciously.

"One could say the same about you, mister," Jessie shot back.

The man seemed surprised, and lowered his rifle just a tad. It took Jessie a moment to realize that with the light fading, and bundled up as she was, the man probably had not taken her for a woman. He seemed a bit more relaxed, but still remained cautious. "Didn't mean no offense, ma'am. We don't get many travelers through here."

"We're on our way to the Indian reservation." That seemed to surprise him even more. "We were hoping for a hot meal and a warm place to sleep."

"S' long as there's no guns or whiskey in that wagon there's always room at the table."

"Take a look for yourself," suggested Ki. "Nothing but blankets, provisions, and some tools."

"I trust you, friend." The man lowered his rifle. "I reckon if you truly were runnin' guns up to the Injuns you'd tell me anythin' but you was headin' up to Three Rivers." He extended his hand. "The name's Caldwell, Sam Caldwell. C'mon inside, my boys'll tend to your team."

Dinner with the Caldwells was a warm, friendly affair. Sam's wife Elsa had prepared a hearty stew of garden vegetables and salt pork. Even in the finer restaurants of San Francisco it would have been good fare, and Jessie said so.

Sam Caldwell beamed with pride. "We grow everything right out back, and by next season we should have twice as many hogs."

"You've done all right, Mr. Caldwell," Jessie said with true respect. Men who came into the wilderness and carved

4

a place for themselves and their families always earned Jessie's admiration.

Sam put his arm around his wife. "But I couldn't have done it without my family."

Looking at Elsa Caldwell, Jessie realized his words were not empty flattery. Elsa was a robust woman whose prematurely graying hair and wrinkled hands attested to the rigors of pioneer life. But there was laughter and kindness in her eyes that even the coldest winters and harshest drafts could not kill. Once, she must have looked much like her daughter Sara, with long, straight brown hair and an engaging smile. The two boys favored their father more, and both had curly brown hair. Toby, the oldest at sixteen, was already the spitting image of his father, with his high forehead and broad nose. It was still uncertain how much James, who was all of eight, would look like his pa.

"An' I reckon the house ain't much, but it keeps us warm an' dry." Sam turned to his son. "Next year, me an' Toby are gonna put down a wood floor, and if 'n it's a good year maybe a real glass window or two."

"I know how working the land can be, but I'm sure you'll get around to it all," Jessie assured him. "In no time you'll have a real palace here. You've made a good start. The worst is over."

Sam and his wife exchanged glances. Jessie could feel the tension in the air.

"That's why we're not gonna let anyone run us off."

Jessie wondered what was behind that statement, but was hesitant to pry into their affairs. They had just met, and there was no reason for the Caldwells to trust a stranger. But if she could, she wanted to help. Her thoughts were cut short.

"Was you at the Alamo?" James blurted out with sudden urgency. He had probably just made the connection between Jessie hailing from Texas and his favorite history lesson. "Did you know Davy Crockett?"

"It was a little before my time, James." She could see

5

the disappointment on the child's face. "But when they were young, Ki knew Jim Bowie. They used to play mumblety-peg together."

"Gol-ly!"

Ignoring the surprised look on Ki's face, and spurred on by the smiles of Sam and Elsa, Jessie continued. "Why, he was the one who taught Jim to throw a knife." Somehow it didn't seem like the lie it was. There was no doubt in Jessie's mind that if Ki had known the legendary Bowie, he probably could have taught him a thing or two about knife-throwing. Her mind wandered even a bit further. "And James," she continued in a conspirator's tone, "had Ki been at the Alamo, things might have gone quite a bit differently." She actually believed that herself.

James's mouth dropped open and he looked at Ki with awe and admiration. Jessie was curious to see how Ki would respond, his policy of honesty now in serious jeopardy. Surprisingly, Ki ignored the boy and turned to the father instead. "Do you have problems with coyotes?"

"Why do you ask?" Sam became suddenly serious.

"There's something out there spooking the horses." The room became silent, and after a moment the faint whinny of the horses could be heard.

"Toby, go out an' check on the animals. Excuse us." They left the table, and Jessie noticed that Sam grabbed the Winchester as he stepped outside.

Elsa continued to question Jessie about big-city ways and the latest fashions, but the conversation was forced and strained. It seemed more out of politeness to her guests than out of real interest that she kept the topic going. Clearly, she was preoccupied with whatever danger might be facing her home and family.

It wasn't long before Sam and Toby returned. They looked none too happy. "There's something out there all right, Ki, but I don't think it's coyotes. Sara, put James to bed." When the two youngest had left the room Sam turned back to his guests. "I'm sorry to get you caught up in all

6

this, but I reckon you'll be a lot safer in here than out there."

"Caught up in what, Mr. Caldwell?" Jessie asked.

A dry chuckle escaped his lips. "It's been happenin' so regular now, I forget there are folks that don't know what's goin' on." He paused, almost not knowing how to put it into words.

Elsa turned to Ki. "Those ain't coyotes, Ki, they're Indians."

Sam nodded his head. "We got Indian problems. Comanches!"

The word had a strange dizzying effect on Jessie, and she suddenly felt like a little girl. Vague memories lost to her conscious mind rushed through her. The Comanches had a special meaning to anyone growing up on the Texas frontier. The Circle Star did not suffer much at the hands of the Indians. Jessie liked to think that was due to Alex Starbuck's fair treatment of his Comanche neighbors, but in truth it had little to do with any sign of respect for her father, and more to do with the fortification of the ranch house, and the veritable army of ranch hands that were always nearby. It was wiser for the Indians to prey on the weaker ranchers than go up against the might of the Starbuck empire. Though Jessie had experienced few firsthand incidents with marauding Indians, there'd been plenty of stories told about the gruesome raids. But there *was* that one night that the Comanche leader Nokoni and his band of Kwahadi braves came swooping down on the Circle Star. . . .

"Jessie, are you all right?" Ki asked with concern.

Jessie was startled. "Oh, I'm, ah . . ."

"You look pale as a ghost."

"I'm fine, Ki."

"You can go an' lie down with Sara and James if you'd like," Sam suggested.

"That won't be necessary," Jessie answered, her color

now back to normal. "I was just thinking of a night very much like this. It was long ago."

Sam Caldwell seemed to understand and said nothing. But Elsa was still concerned about her guest. "If gunfire'll upset you, you might be better off in the back."

That brought a smile to Ki's face. "Don't count her out so quickly," he said, the grin still plastered to his face. "She might be a better shot than anyone in this room."

Sam nodded his head. "Now, it may not come down to that. They may be riding through, or they may just sneak in an' steal a chicken or two."

"Sometimes we let 'em go in an' take what they want. S'long as they don't do it too often or take too much. We don't want no trouble," Elsa explained to no one in particular.

"Maybe I'll go out and check on our wagon."

"Hold it, Ki. It may be nothin', but then again, no one can say fer sure. You'd best stay inside."

Ki turned to Jessie, but the question was soon resolved. Gunshots rang out in the night.

"Douse the lamps," Sam ordered. But Elsa was already doing it.

From nowhere, Toby came in and handed Jessie a powerful Sharp's rifle. "If you're as good a shot as Ki says, you should have this."

"You keep it, Toby. It has a bit too much of a kick for me." She crossed over to where her jacket hung on a peg, and pulled out her cordovan leather holster from the large side pocket. She unrolled the gunbelt and gripped the custom-made, slate-gray Colt .38 by its polished peach-wood handle.

The beauty of the weapon did not go unnoticed. Toby let out an appreciative "Wow," and added, "I reckon you *are* as good as Ki says."

Jessie winked at him. "Let's get into position."

"Toby, you an' Jessie take the far window, me an' Ki

8

got this one. And don't start firin' till your eyes 'come accustomed to the dark."

"Right, Pa."

The heavy wooden shutters had a tiny slat in them that, when opened, gave enough room for a clear shot, yet offered a fair amount of protection for the rifleman. Jessie and Toby knelt by the crack and waited for their eyes to adjust.

"Sure is black out there," Toby stated plainly.

Jessie looked up at the sky. It was an overcast night; not a single star could be seen. "I thought the Comanches wouldn't attack on a moonless night."

"Don't really know. That may have been true once, but now they've learned a lot from other tribes. I've heard some say you can't tell one tribe from another these days, they're all actin' so alike."

Sam and Ki, using one of the Caldwells' revolvers, began firing from their window. "Can't really see clear, but we can't let 'em march right up to the door," Sam called out.

"Right, Pa." Toby began firing out the window, and Jessie did the same. Soon the room was filled with acrid gunsmoke. "Whatever they're up to they're stayin' pretty far back, Pa."

"They're showing their respect for that Big Fifty," Jessie said as she motioned to Toby's rifle. The large boom of the Sharp's could not be mistaken for anything else. It went without saying what a gun that could down a buffalo could do to a man. But what a white man understood as simple respect, an Indian interpreted as fear. And it was unlike a Comanche to show fear of anything, especially in battle.

Sam kept cocking and firing his Winchester as fast as possible. "Keep firin', Toby, I think we might be scarin' them off."

Jessie didn't think a Comanche war party could be scared off. When braves set out on a raid, only insurmountable odds would turn them from their task. Jessie looked around the room. Even with the powerful Sharp's, this hardly seemed like insurmountable odds. But she kept her thoughts to herself.

Jessie noticed it first, but the others in the room quickly noticed it as well; the shooting outside the house had stopped. Sam put down his gun. "Maybe they was just plannin' on givin' us a scare."

"Or maybe they got more than they bargained for. We do got two more guns than usual, Pa."

"Could be, but either way I'm glad it's over." Sam let out a relaxed sigh. "I don't think they'll be back tonight. Why don't you folks try an' get some sleep? I'll stay up and keep watch."

"I'll keep you company, Sam," Ki offered.

"No need. If anything looks suspicious I'll wake you."

"Come on, Jessie. I'll put you in with Sara." Elsa took Jessie by the arm, then turned to Ki. "And I'll set you up a cot by the hearth. Sleep well."

As Elsa led her off, that odd look returned to Jessie's face. She turned to Ki, but she could have been addressing anyone. "I may be wrong, but I don't think they fired a single arrow."

Chapter 2

When Ki woke at the first sign of light, Sam Caldwell was already up and about. Ki dressed hurriedly and, as a courtesy to the others, fired up the kitchen stove before going out to scour the land. He wasn't certain what he was looking for, but something in Jessie's last comment had aroused his curiosity. It was quite reasonable for the Indians to abandon a traditional weapon like the bow and arrow in favor of the more modern and effective rifle, but if Jessie had an odd feeling about the Indian attack, Ki wanted to have a look for himself. Intuition sometimes had a way of finding the flaws in an otherwise logical scenario. Ki had his own questions as well. Usually any attacking band left a calling card of sorts, either to take credit for the action or to instill further terror and expand their reputation. Often the cartel had left their insignia on a piece of handiwork as a direct challenge to the Starbuck empire. A lance embedded deeply in the door would proclaim a warrior's bravery, and serve as the band's "calling card." On a moonless night any Indian could have sneaked up within throwing range. Unless, of course, one had tried and subsequently been shot down.

"I don't think you'll find any souvenirs." Carrying a bucket of chicken feed, Sam walked out from the shed to join Ki. Ki smiled politely. He wasn't sure whether Sam was making a joke or being serious. "I already looked for bodies, but it's no use. The Comanches always carry off their dead an' wounded."

"Any signs of blood?" Ki asked.

Sam shook his head. "But then I ain't the best sign reader," he said almost apologetically.

"On hard ground like this it's difficult," Ki explained. Even with his experience he didn't know if he could piece together a good picture of what had happened here last night.

"Once they left behind a dead pony. A broken shank, they had to shoot it."

"Has there been much trouble with gunrunners?" Ki asked without raising his eyes from the ground.

"None that I know of," Sam answered.

That brought a puzzled look from Ki. "Then what made you think . . . ?"

"How else would the Injuns get their guns?" It was a good question, and Ki had no answer for it. "You were here last night," Sam added with unnecessary emphasis.

"And that's why I'd like to get a few things straight. If there were only a few braves it may not be a serious problem."

"You wouldn't say that if you lived here, Ki," protested Sam.

"No, of course not. I don't mean to make out like it's been easy for you."

"It hasn't been."

"What I meant was a few hostile braves could always get their hands on some rifles. But if there's somebody running guns to the Indians, the problem could be much worse."

Sam nodded his head in understanding. "Still, I don't think you'll find many answers out here, and I got chores to do."

Ki was about a quarter of a mile from the house when

12

he found what he was looking for. There, in the low buffalo grass, were four distinct sets of hoofprints.

After breakfast they all said warm farewells. They had met as strangers, but after only one night parted as close friends. The hazards of frontier life often did that. The possibility of death and the need to band together to ward off destruction formed many a close bond.

As Elsa and Jessie hugged good-bye Jessie whispered softly, "Now remember, if you ever need help don't hesitate to call. We'll be at the reservation." Elsa squeezed her a little tighter. "And any time in the future, you can get word to us at the Circle Star."

"Thank you, Jessie. Now you take care."

Toby had the wagon hitched up and waiting. Ki said his good-byes and made sure to shake James's hand before climbing up and taking the reins. Jessie slipped into the seat next to him.

Elsa turned to her husband. "Maybe Toby should ride with them. Those Injuns might still be lurkin' about."

Sam seemed to be considering the idea. "Don't be silly," Jessie said quickly. "There are chores to get done. We'll be fine."

"Another gun never hurts, Jessie. Chores can always wait," Sam said unselfishly.

Jessie broke into a huge grin. "Now I know that's not true, Sam Caldwell," she admonished playfully. "Remember, I'm a rancher myself. But thank you." She patted Ki's arm. "Ki is all the protection I need. Don't you worry." Ki gave a quick flick of the reins and a soft "Giddyap," and the wagon was on its way.

As they traveled northwest, the topography began to slowly change. It was for the most part still flat plains, but the land here was dotted with more trees and in the near distance small hillocks sprung up to break the monotony of the smooth horizon. It was a cold morning, but the sun had

13

warmed the air enough for Jessie to remove her brown Stetson. Her tawny bronze hair fell down to her shoulders.

"I didn't want to discuss it in front of the Caldwells, but about last night . . ." Ki began without any preamble.

"I don't exactly know what came over me, Ki. But I don't think it'll happen again. We've dealt with Indians enough in the past, and I've never had any kind of problem before."

"I know that Jessie, but—"

"Let me finish. If they were bad Indians they were no different than any other cartel plug-uglies. And if they were law-abiding, I treated them like anyone else."

"I know that, Jessie, but—" Ki tried again, but Jessie persisted.

"There was just something so reminiscent about last night, the small room, the fear in the air, the feeling of desperation. It was like the scariest dream I had as a little girl, but it wasn't a dream this time."

"Jessie, we don't have to talk about it, if you don't want to."

"There's nothing much to talk about. I can't really remember the dream too clearly." Jessie paused briefly, then continued. "When I was very young, there was a ranch hand who used to tell stories about raiding Comanches and burned-out settlements. He was quite a yarn spinner, very prone to exaggeration, but of course as a little girl I never realized it." She paused again, perhaps thinking of one of the better tales.

"It's the same everywhere," Ki interjected softly. "There was an old farmer who used to tell me about the brigands that would sweep through his village every harvest."

"This ranch hand would scare the dickens out of me," Jessie recalled, "but I'd always go back to hear another one. He made them seem so real and so alive. And last night could have been one of his stories."

"Luckily, it wasn't."

"I know. But for a moment there . . ." Jessie let out a

14

little chuckle. "After years of running from an imaginary bogeyman, to one day find that bogeyman practically knocking on your door." She gave a quick shudder.

With a sigh, Ki nodded. "I can understand."

"Good. Because I wouldn't want you to think I'm scared of Indians."

"Jessie," Ki blurted out, "those weren't Indians!"

"What?"

"That's what I've been trying to tell you. I wasn't referring to your behavior last night, I was—"

"And you let me go on and on."

Ki smiled. "I tried to stop you."

"I was just rambling on like a scared pup, and you . . ." She felt herself getting hot under the collar and knew she must be blushing. She turned to look the other way.

"All I wanted to say was I don't think those were Indians attacking last night." Ki let a minute pass, then added, "I thought you might be interested in knowing *why* I don't think they were Indians."

"I'm sure you have your reasons, Ki," she said with mock anger.

"I do," replied Ki. "But don't you want to know what made me suspicious?"

"Undoubtedly," she began with heavy sarcasm, "it was your inscrutable Oriental intuition."

"Not exactly. It was your intuition, Jessie."

"Mine?"

Ki nodded. "If you felt something was amiss, I thought I had better investigate."

"Did you now," Jessie said with just the slightest trace of amusement. Ki nodded. "And what did you find?" continued Jessie.

"Horse tracks. Probably four horses. But that's not important. What is important is the tracks were side by side."

Jessie already understood. "It all makes sense now. I think."

"Attacking on a moonless night, no arrows, being run off so easily. All that is circumstantial."

"Because Indians never ride abreast of each other," concluded Jessie.

"It's true," agreed Ki. "Only white men ride that way. Indians don't talk as they ride, and they don't want their trail to give away how many are in their party."

"But then that means—" Jessie stopped herself short. She wasn't quite sure what it meant. And this was no longer the time to ponder it. From off to their right, a dust cloud began to grow. "Ki," she said urgently, and pointed.

"I see it, Jessie, and, Indians or not, we're going to give them a run for their money." He snapped the reins smartly and let out a little whoop. The team jumped into a gallop and the buckboard sprang forward.

Although the dust cloud was still some distance away, it was approaching at an ever-increasing rate, and it didn't take long to realize that the heavily laden wagon would soon be overtaken. The pursuers were coming on at an angle that in no time would head off the wagon.

"I'm going to try and keep as much distance as possible between us and them," Ki shouted over the pounding of the hooves and squeaking of the buckboard. "Hang on!" With that, Ki steered the wagon off the trail.

Jessie hung on for dear life. At the speed they were going every rock, every groove, every mound of dirt was a teeth-jarring obstacle threatening to throw her from the wagon. The springboard, which ordinarily cushioned the ride over bad terrain, was now having quite the opposite effect. The otherwise gentle, flexing motion that would absorb shock was now, due to the increased speed, acting more like a trampoline, continuously bouncing Jessie up and out of the seat.

"Ki, I'll never be able to get a shot off like this."

"We don't know who we're going to be shooting at yet, Jessie," was Ki's reply.

Ki had been concentrating intently on guiding the

16

wagon, and had his eyes focused forward. Jessie, though, turned around. "That's not exactly true." The gap between hunter and hunted was closing rapidly. Jessie could clearly make out the fringed deerskin leggings and the feathered lance of the lead rider. "They're Indians!"

"How many?"

"Looks like five." Jessie had to yell to be heard. "Maybe we should just pull up and make a stand."

"Let's try to make that ridge." Ki nodded his head toward a low ridge off to the left.

"Easy for you to say. You have more weight keeping you in the seat."

"Just hang on. Weight has nothing to do with it." Ki was hardly even sitting on the wagon seat. He had adopted the "horse stance," a basic martial-arts fighting position. His feet were planted a little more than shoulder width apart, his knees were bent, and his back straight. His bottom barely touched the wagon seat. But his center of gravity was greatly lowered. He imagined his feet were nailed to the floorboard of the wagon. By making very slight adjustments and subtle shifts in his balance he was able to maintain a stable position.

"If I don't make it, pick me up on the way back," Jessie said between clenched teeth.

"We're just about there."

Jessie turned to keep an eye on the approaching Indians. True to his word, they were soon over the ridge, and Ki was bringing the wagon to a sudden stop. Jessie was still facing the rear when she felt Ki's restraining arm. "Don't make a move; turn around slowly."

Jessie knew better than to question Ki. She did as he said, then immediately understood why. Blocking the path of the wagon were a dozen mounted Comanche braves.

"If they wanted us dead, they wouldn't be sitting there waiting patiently."

"I know," agreed Jessie. "By now we'd both look like overgrown pincushions." Jessie didn't move a muscle, though she kept thinking of the Colt .38 that was tucked away in her jacket pocket. "But then what do they want?" she wondered out loud.

"I'm sure we'll find out soon enough," answered Ki.

Jessie began to study the Indians, but she was soon distracted by the pounding of horses at her back. The other five Indians had caught up with their prey. Although there was no possible way to escape, the fact that they were now totally surrounded made the back of Jessie's neck crawl. She turned around and continued to examine their would-be captors. She could see why many ignorant white folks thought "all Injuns look alike." All the braves had the same copper-colored skin and dark, thick hair, and there was no doubt they came from the same basic stock, with their round foreheads, thin lips, and aquiline noses. They were all dressed similarly in buckskin shirts and leggings, though some had thin hides wrapped around their waists, while others had wool blankets. Her eyes came to rest on one brave who carried a long lance. She gave a little shudder. Was that a human scalp or horsehair that hung from the wooden shaft? His hair was not tied in a ponytail like the others, but was drawn back from his forehead, and then hung down loose past his shoulders. Besides the fact that he carried the lance, something in his posture made Jessie suspect he was the leader of the small band.

Jessie's intuition was not wrong. When he jabbed the spear silently in the air, two of the other Indians closed in on the wagon and began rifling through the buckboard's cargo. They threw the contents around roughly but apparently did not find what they were looking for. One of the Indians let out a monosyllable: *"Ge"*— Comanche for "nothing."

"Perhaps if you tell us what you are looking for we could help," Jessie said boldly. There was no reaction to her words; she half-expected none. Among the Plains Indians many languages were spoken and there were as many dialects as there were tribes, but Comanche was almost a

18

universal language. Many of their words were basic and translated accurately, or reasonably so. Jessie had gone out of her way to learn a few fundamental phrases. *"Hahn haints"*—"greetings"—she said now. The Comanche leader seemed to show some interest. Jessie pointed to Ki and herself and continued, *"tasha."*

Immediately the braves began to laugh raucously. Jessie felt stung by the insult. But then one of the Indians threw back his head and let out a loud howl. The laughter increased and soon others joined him in his howling. Jessie's embarrassment flared into anger. "How dare you! No wonder people think of you as savages. We come in peace as friends and . . ."

The Comanche leader stopped laughing. "We do not think you are coyote," he said calmly. "Maybe you are friend, maybe no, but you are not coyote." Again there was another howl, and this time she recognized the howl to be an imitation of a coyote.

Even Ki began to chuckle. "I'm not sure, Jessie, but I don't think you actually said what you thought you said." Jessie glared at Ki, outraged that he seemed to have joined in the joke. "It's happened to me too, when I first learned English," he hastened to add.

Her anger was not abated though, and she turned back to the Comanche. "You speak the white man's tongue," she said almost accusingly.

The Indian shook his head. "The white man speaks with forked tongue. I speak the white man's words. Nothing more."

"Then you understand we come in peace, as friends."

"We understand you and you"—he pointed to Ki as well—"are *tasha.*" He let out a small howl, but continued without further laughter: *"Tesha,* friend, *tasha . . ."* He threw back his head once more and howled softly.

"I think you told them we're coyotes," Ki said with a smile.

"I may have been a bit slow, Ki, but I think I got the

joke now." Jessie was obviously still smarting from being made the butt of their amusement.

"There is no disgrace, do not feel bitter," the Comanche said with a smile. "Not many whites learn the *numinu* tongue."

Jessie recognized the Indian name for Comanche. Literally translated it meant "the people." That was how the Comanches referred to themselves. "We come as friends and should speak as *tesha*," she said, careful this time with the pronunciation. "Friends do not ambush friends."

The leader nodded. "Because you learn Comanche words does not make you friend. Many white man say 'friend' to trick Indian. True friend does not give crazy water to Indians, then steal his buffalo hides."

"Whiskey runners," Ki said almost to himself. He turned to Jessie. "They're checking to see if we're smuggling whiskey onto the reservation."

The Indian nodded at the mention of whiskey. "Black Elk say the white man's poison bad for braves. Colonel McKenzie and his yellow stockings say Indians prohibited from drinking whiskey, but still the white man brings whiskey to the Indians."

"We have only blankets and tools for the Indians." Jessie gestured to the back of the wagon.

"If the white man did not kill all our buffalo we would have no need for your thin blankets." The Indian spat out the words. "But since you come with offerings for the Comanche we take what we need." He gave another gesture and two of the braves rode over to the rear of the wagon, where Jessie and Ki's saddle horses, a young sorrel and an older bay, were tethered. The braves began to untie the reins.

"Wait a minute, those are our horses," Jessie protested. As she swung around her tawny hair glistened in the sunlight. The nearer of the two braves reached out and caught a lock of her hair. He barely had time to feel it between his

20

fingers before Ki's fist caught him in the mouth and knocked him from his horse.

Ki leaped from the wagon and crashed headfirst into the other brave. They both tumbled to the ground. Ki sprang to his feet quickly, and turned to face the first brave. The Indian stood opposite him, a long hunting knife drawn and at the ready.

As soon as Jessie realized what was happening, she reached for her revolver. But before her hand could clear her jacket pocket, the Comanche leader had his lance just inches from her neck.

Her fingers let the gun drop.

Chapter 3

The war chief barked out a command and the brave froze where he stood. There was a particularly high-spirited conversation between the two that ended with the leader nodding his head. He turned to Jessie. "Dark Cloud meant you no harm. He never saw hair that glistened like the setting of the sun. His only desire was to touch the medicine that made it so."

"Tell Dark Cloud I take no offense by his action." Jessie chose her words carefully. Honor was everything among the proud Comanches. She held out a lock of hair to him. "He may feel it again, if he'd like." She wondered, though, if her gesture was like throwing a bone to a hungry wolf who was quite capable of taking the whole meal.

The warrior stood firm, and the leader explained. "It is not a simple matter. To be struck by a . . ."—he hesitated a moment before finding the proper word— "white halfbreed is a serious offense to his honor."

Jessie was impressed by the chief's observation and exactness. Most whites took Ki for a total Oriental. "But he was only trying to protect me," she explained. "Wouldn't Dark Cloud have done the same?"

The war chief smiled. "I have told him just that, but it makes no difference. His honor is at stake. His honor must be restored."

"We have many gifts we can offer." She gestured to the back of the wagon.

The leader looked to Dark Cloud. With or without an understanding of English, the gist of Jessie's comment was clear. Dark Cloud folded his arms across his chest. "There is only one gift that will restore his honor," the leader said solemnly. "Your friend's life."

The words left Jessie speechless. "You can't just kill a man in cold blood because . . ." she began in protest.

"To kill an unarmed man is the white man's way. They will meet each other in combat."

That left Jessie feeling only a little better. She had no doubts that Ki could handle himself in most situations, and given a one-to-one confrontation she would bet almost anything that Ki would come out the victor, but that in itself was the problem. Was it likely that a band of hot-blooded Comanche warriors would let a white halfbreed first insult one of their own, then add insult to injury or, more precisely, injury to insult by letting him beat the brave in a fight? Any further humiliation at the hands of Ki could cost them their lives. But what choice did Ki have?

Ki must have been wondering the very same thing. Up till now he had been silent, content to let Jessie handle the negotiations, but it was all too clear where things were heading. He gave a short bow to the offended Comanche. "I ask your forgiveness. I meant you no disgrace. I acted, without thought, my only purpose to protect the woman."

"Dark Cloud understands some of your words, but as you speak of matters of importance I will translate."

"Thank you," Ki said.

Unmoved, Dark Cloud listened to the translation. He felt his swollen, discolored jaw, then spat out blood. There was no need for the Comanche leader to interpret Dark Cloud's gesture. Ki spoke again. "I am a halfbreed. I have the powers of both my mother and father. My mother came from a land far away across the great lake, the Pacific Ocean. It was in this place, called the Japans, that I was

23

born." Ki assumed that the Comanches, like other tribes, had a fondness and a regard for folktales and legend.

His words were translated, then Dark Cloud made a brief comment. "Dark Cloud says it is sad that you will die in a land so far from that of your birth."

"I have learned the white man's way, and this is as much my home. But I have also learned the magic of Japan. A land where warriors are honored above all others. Their power is so great that even the white man runs from the mighty samurai." He was certain they would respect power and magic.

"Are you one of these samurai?" the war chief asked, pronouncing the word with great effort.

Ki shook his head. "A halfbreed could never be a true samurai."

"That must bring great disgrace to your ancestors," the Comanche replied.

For the second time Jessie found herself surprised by these "savages." Bloodthirsty as they might be, they showed a certain sensitivity in matters of honor and familial responsibility. She also wondered where Ki was going with his tale. Surely he couldn't expect to talk his way out of this simply by explaining his ancestry.

"I was an outcast," replied Ki. "But it only made my magic stronger, the way an arrowhead is strengthened by fire and water."

The Comanche nodded, and conveyed Ki's meaning with words and a gesture with his lance. Dark Cloud said a few words, then pressed his knife point into his own forearm. "Your strength may be great, but your blood will still spill from the point of his blade," came the translation.

Ki shook his head. "My medicine is great. The blade will not penetrate my flesh." Ki realized that mere talk would not dissuade Dark Cloud, but if he could adopt a solid air of utter confidence the Indian might have second thoughts. "I have lived and studied with the great medicine men of my land. Men so powerful and wise they live in

24

great temples, and even the mighty rulers of the land pay them homage.

"We have our own medicine men, but they have not stopped the white men from enslaving our people."

Sudden insight hit Ki. "My medicine can defeat even the strongest warrior. My medicine harnesses the power of the land, the sun, and the moon. It uses the power of the creatures that walk the land and fly in the sky." He gestured broadly with his arms. As his words were translated he could see they had their effect. As with the best legends, this statement contained some truth. The basis of all the martial arts involved focusing the energy that was within all living things, the ever-present *ki*. It was only a simple extension to include the power of the sun and moon. The Chinese martial arts also had their basis in the fighting movements of the many animals. Ki continued. "My medicine encompasses the striking force of the eagle, and the might of the bear."

That should do it, Jessie thought to herself. Indians had great reverence for the power of animal spirits.

Dark Cloud began to speak. *"Tasha . . . ?"*

"There are no coyotes in my land across the ocean," Ki interrupted, without waiting for the interpreter. "There is an animal more cunning and more powerful than the coyote." He waited for the translation, then continued. "He is called 'tiger.' His strength is captured in the medicine called 'Tiger's Claw,'" Ki said.

That led to a brief discussion among the Indians. "We have never heard a white man talk as you. Truly you are a man of medicine. But that does not change anything. You will fight."

Ki continued undaunted. "The spirit of the tiger lives in me." He took a deep breath, expanding his chest noticeably. Then, with a quick contraction of his diaphragm, he forced the air up and through his vocal cords. The result was a thundering roar. He timed it with a fast rake of his hand, shaped like an extended claw, through the air. The

25

action took everyone by surprise, and the Indian ponies reared back.

Dark Cloud, though his countenance seemed a bit pale, took up a fighting stance. He spoke quickly and his words were translated. "You are not a simple man. You have the spirit of the animal in you. A man like you does not need a weapon. We will fight, and we will fight now. It will be a great honor to defeat a man with the spirit of this tiger."

It appeared as if all of Ki's efforts had backfired. But the Indian's confidence was shaken; he believed in Ki's spiritual powers. That could have some benefit. But there was no time to dwell on that now. Dark Cloud had his blade ready and could strike at any moment. Ki quickly shed his jacket. The initial chill would stiffen his muscles and slow his reactions, but as his energy flowed and warmed his body it would be less of a hindrance than the bulky jacket. The thick sheepskin would also offer some protection from the Comanche's knife, but Ki had no intention of letting the blade get close to him.

Ki studied his opponent. On looks alone Dark Cloud did not seem a formidable threat. Like most Comanches he was of medium height, and had a slightly squat build. On foot the Comanche had none of the grace they were so famed for while on horseback. But the most important factor, and the one that established Dark Cloud as a skilled fighter, was the way he held his knife. Most whites, and unskilled fighters, held a knife palm up and underhand, and tended to use their forearm to slash and jab the point. That not only limited their movements but made it easier either to knock the knife away or trap the knife hand. A proficient knife fighter grasped the knife in his fist and wielded it overhand. That gave a much stronger grip, and made the movement of the blade much more dangerous. It not only did more damage on impact, but was also harder to predict and block against. The fist could be used as in any fight, but a hook, cross, backfist, or even a block could have disastrous effects if contact was made.

26

Dark Cloud circled Ki with his knife held in a firm overhand grip. Ki noted that the Indian's arm length was a few inches shorter than his own. That would have been a significant factor if Ki intended to fight the Comanche on equal terms. But he did not. He was well aware that defeating the Indian might not be the end of the problem.

Suddenly Dark Cloud came at him, shooting his knife hand out in front. Instinctively, Ki grabbed the wrist, ducked under the arm, and came up behind Dark Cloud. A swift push sent the off-balance Indian into the dirt.

Dark Cloud gained his feet quickly and shook his head. No doubt he had intended to grapple it out with Ki, relying on his strength and the extra edge the knife gave him. Ki's evasive maneuvers left him puzzled. And that gave Ki what he hoped would be the solution. If he could continue to evade Dark Cloud, making as little contact with him as possible, the Indian might accept Ki's spiritual superiority and call off the contest without fear of further disgrace. A combination of Ninja gymnastics and *jujutsu* might do the trick.

Dark Cloud was a fast learner. This time he came in low, making sure Ki would not be able to dodge under his blade. Ki did the next-best thing. He flexed his powerful thighs and somersaulted high over the head of the surprised Indian.

As Ki landed nimbly on his toes the Comanche was already rushing headlong toward him. The threat of the blade made the timing of Ki's next move critical. Once he had a firm grip on Dark Cloud's knife hand, he could drop to his back and send the Indian flying over his head. He just had to keep his eye on the wrist. . . .

It took surprisingly little effort to hurl the Indian into the air. The art of *jujutsu* was centered on turning your opponent's own strength and momentum against him. The fact that the Indian had probably never seen such fighting tactics in either the red or white man's combat styles made him an almost eager accomplice. Dark Cloud came in again with the very same move, to the very same result.

Another feint, and then a backfist with the blade. When the point arrived Ki was already in midair where a back flip took him safely out of the range of the knife. When he landed, Dark Cloud was angrily screaming at the war chief. The Indian leader nodded and gracefully slid down from his horse. He pulled out a knife from his sheath, and approached Ki. Ki tensed, preparing to take on both Indians at once. Seeing his reaction, the war chief smiled, turned the knife around, and grasped it by the blade. He offered the weapon, handle first, to Ki. "Dark Cloud can understand your fear. You are unarmed. Maybe your medicine is not as great as we thought. Maybe you are not as powerful as you say."

"My medicine is even more powerful than I have told you," Ki said as he took the knife. "I do not need this weapon. If I intended Dark Cloud harm he would not be standing there now." This was not an idle boast; Ki spoke the truth.

His absolute confidence must have convinced the Comanche leader. "Running Wolf does not wish to see a brave warrior die in needless combat," he said craftily, with no indication of which warrior he felt might come to harm. "If you can show me your great power I will end the combat."

Ki understood what he was looking for. Some sign that would leave them all convinced that Ki was not a mortal being made of flesh and blood but the earthly embodiment of a great spirit. A few tricks came to mind, but Ki quickly dismissed them as being just that: tricks. Finally he shook his head and spoke slowly. "My spirit says its power is not to be mocked. It is not to be paraded about for the amusement of old women and children."

"Your spirit has great wisdom," the chief said solemnly. "That is how it should be. There are too many false spirits."

For a moment Ki thought it might have been a test question, one that he had inadvertently answered correctly. But as the Indian continued he realized there was nothing more

28

than simple respect in the war chief's words. "Still you will fight," the Comanche said as he pulled a leather thong from around his waist. He knelt down and tied one end of the strap around Dark Cloud's ankle. "Your spirit may flee but your flesh will stay and fight."

It was clear what he intended to do with the other end of the strap. Ki noticed the other Indians moved their horses into a circle around the two combatants. Running Wolf extended his arm, waiting for Ki to bring his foot forward. Ki looked around and realized he had no choice. He stepped forward with his left foot, then changed his mind and placed his right foot in front. The lash was tied tightly to his ankle. "If you cut the thong before the fight is over you will die," the chief said simply as he stood up and stepped back.

"My spirit is angered that you shackle my body this way," Ki said. "An angered spirit bodes evil for Dark Cloud."

"Then it will be," Dark Cloud said in hesitant English.

"You speak English," Ki said with surprise. Obviously it was an unnecessary comment, but Ki was trying to buy time. With only a few feet separating them he would need to employ different tactics. He could no longer hope to avoid the Indian's knife without physical contact.

"A little."

"I mean you no harm, Dark Cloud," Ki explained once more.

"I die or you die, Spirit HalfBreed."

"It doesn't have to be, Dark Cloud." Ki was still stalling for time. At this point he didn't think he could convince the Indian not to fight, but he needed time to figure out how he would deal with the thong, and the close infighting that would ensue.

"You will bring my family much pride."

"You underestimate my spirit, Dark Cloud. My spirit will not allow itself to be used for your glory." The sentence was a little too complex for Dark Cloud's English, and he turned to his leader for an interpretation. While his words were being translated, Ki continued his scheming. It was essential to keep as much distance between himself and the warrior. That meant he would have to use his one free leg to keep Dark Cloud at bay.

"There is no other way. I die or you die," Dark Cloud repeated. "At the fire my family will talk of this day."

Ki had built his image too well. Dead or alive, Dark Cloud would only be honored by his duel to the death with the legendary Spirit HalfBreed. Then it hit Ki. If he could only pin the Comanche long enough to use his knowledge of atemi.... The art of applying pressure to certain points on the body to render an opponent unconscious was perfect when sneaking up on unsuspecting victims, but during a struggle it would be difficult to find the chance to apply the necessary pressure to the right points. Of course, Ki could simply try to beat the Indian to a pulp, stopping just short of death. But tied together, he wasn't certain he could accomplish that without the Indian getting in one lucky, and possibly deadly, thrust of his blade.

At first Ki hoped to turn his tethered leg to his advantage by using the thong to sweep the Indian right off his feet. But this hope faded as his opponent began to circle. The Comanche kept his feet evenly spaced apart and his knees bent in a somewhat looser version of the "horse stance" Ki had employed earlier to maintain his position during the wildly bucking wagon ride.

From the deadly look of concentration in Dark Cloud's eyes, Ki knew his time for further thought had come to an end. The Indian might strike at any time. Only the weapon in Ki's hand kept Dark Cloud from rushing in immediately. If, unarmed, the Spirit HalfBreed could handle Dark Cloud, then a knife-wielding Spirit HalfBreed demanded a moment's consideration.

But that was all Ki got before Dark Cloud struck. The Comanche moved to close the distance, and Ki reacted like lightning. His free leg shot out and snapped into the Indian's solar plexus. Dark Cloud doubled over, gasping, momentarily paralyzed by the powerful and unsuspected blow. He didn't even get a chance to catch his breath. Ki saw his opening and took it.

Without bringing back his leg Ki hooked it over Dark Cloud's head, then snapped his leg down. The Indian dropped like a felled tree. As he hit the ground Ki shot his knee onto the Indian's chest, pinning him under his weight. Ki let go of his knife and used both hands to deliver two simultaneous spear-hand strikes to the base of the Indian's jaw. Ki's fingertips pressed into the vital atemi points that lay in the soft spot where the jaw met the skull under the earlobe. The Comanche went slack in a sudden faint.

Ki picked up his knife and slashed through the leather thong. He stood up slowly. The other Comanches seemed dazed that the fight had ended. One Indian slid off his horse and went to the unconscious Dark Cloud. The moment of truth had come. Ki thought his words out carefully. "My spirit has taken Dark Cloud's spirit. When you are gone and my spirit can no longer be angered by your sight, the spirit of Dark Cloud will again enter his body."

That created a brief stir among the Indians. Running Wolf instructed the others to place Dark Cloud back on his horse and lash him in place. When that was done he turned to Ki. "You have a powerful spirit," he said slowly, "but not as powerful as you would have us believe." He brought his lance up to Ki's rib cage. "Look."

Under his arm, Ki's shirt was discolored. Only now did Ki feel the warm, sticky blood that flowed from the cut in his side. As Dark Cloud went down his flailing arm must have caught Ki in the side.

Meanwhile the Comanche leader grabbed the reins of Jessie and Ki's saddle horses. The other Indians started to ride out.

"You're stealing our horses," protested Jessie.

"And you trespass on our land, Hair Like Setting Sun," the Comanche replied, as he kicked his horse into a trot.

31

The Indians were gone in an instant, leaving a faint dust cloud in their wake.

Jessie hopped down from the wagon and rushed over to Ki. "Are you all right? Let me take a look at that."

"It's not as bad as it looks," assured Ki. "It's just a scratch."

Jessie gave him a reproachful look. "Take off your shirt," she insisted.

"I'll probably freeze to death from the cold long before I bleed to death, Jessie." Still Ki did as he was told.

"I guess I believe you," Jessie said once she saw that the skin was just grazed and the blood was already starting to clot over. "Then why in hell didn't you stop them from taking our horses?" Jessie handed the startled Ki his jacket.

"Should I have fought them all?" Ki wondered out loud.

"Why didn't you tell them your spirit would haunt them forever if they took our horses?" she said with a playful chide to her voice.

Ki laughed. "Just wasn't thinking."

"I wouldn't say that, Ki. That was a pretty good yarn you told, and it was a masterful fight. A nice variation on a double kick."

"Thank you," Ki said as they climbed into the wagon.

"As a matter of fact, a move that smooth and effective was almost worth the price of the two horses."

"Thank you," Ki repeated with a bit of a grin.

"I said 'almost.'" There was a twinkle in Jessie's eyes as she flicked the reins and started the team moving.

They had only gone a short way before Jessie turned to Ki. "When do you think we'll hit the reservation?"

"I can't be sure, but I think we already have," Ki answered.

"Then those Comanches weren't renegades?"

"That I don't know. But I do think they were on reservation land."

"Then when Running Wolf accused us of trespassing he was serious."

"I'm sure he was."

Jessie continued, "I thought he was just referring to the white men in general coming and taking Indian lands."

"That, too," Ki said plainly. "Again I can't be certain, but I think we hit Indian land as soon as we got off the high ground."

"Last night?" Jessie asked. Ki nodded. It took a moment to sink in. "But then that means the Caldwells—"

"That's right, Jessie. They're wonderful people, but they're homesteading on the Comanche reservation."

They rode in silence for a moment while Jessie pondered the ramifications of that. This time they noticed the dust cloud at the same time. "Not again," was Jessie's only comment.

"But this time it's no small band," Ki observed. "There must be a dozen riders, at least.

Chapter 4

Before they could decide whether to make a run for it or try to find cover and shoot it out, it became clear that there would be no need for either. The blue-and-yellow banner announced the arrival of the United States Cavalry. There were sixteen riders to be exact, half a troop, coming on in a neat column of twos.

The commanding officer brought the company to a halt and approached the wagon. "Afternoon, sir, ma'am," he said with a tip of his hat. "I'm afraid we're going to have to search your cargo."

"What else is new?" Jessie muttered under her breath.

The officer turned to her, misunderstanding her comment. "You're in Indian Territory, ma'am, and we have to check for smugglers," he explained politely.

"Do you ever check for horse thieves?" Jessie asked dryly.

"Pardon me, ma'am . . . ?" The officer was clearly puzzled.

"Horse thieves, people who take someone's animals without permission." The cavalry officer looked like a scared jackrabbit. Suddenly Jessie changed her tone. "Look, Officer . . . ?"

"Stafford. Lieutenant Mason Stafford, at your service, ma'am," he said with a crisp salute.

"Lieutenant, to put it briefly, we were just stopped by a band of Comanches who stole our horses. So forgive my seemingly rude behavior."

"I understand, ma'am."

"And please stop calling me ma'am. I'm Jessica Starbuck and this is Ki. We're headed for the reservation."

"You're Jessie Starbuck?" the lieutenant blurted out.

"To my friends, yes."

"I didn't mean nothing by it, ma'am—I mean, Miss Star—Mrs. Star—"

Jessie almost hated to rescue the embarrassed lieutenant, but she did nonetheless. "Jessie, please."

The lieutenant smiled and continued with his apology, but Jessie wasn't really listening. Something in the lieutenant's manner had irritated Jessie, but when he smiled she saw the boy inside the man's uniform. His green eyes came alive with his grin, and Jessie could see his businesslike demeanor was just a way of hiding the glee that the little boy felt at being able to sit astride a horse and play cavalry commander. The fact that Mason Stafford was no longer a child but a grown man did not offend Jessie; on the contrary, she was almost attracted by his youthful zeal.

". . . So I had no idea that when Major General Cropsey kept referring to Jessie Starbuck it would turn out to be someone so"—the lieutenant began to blush and dropped his voice shyly—"young an' pretty."

"Why, thank you, Lieutenant."

"Please call me Stafford."

"But you expected an old battle-ax?" Jessie finished.

Stafford nodded. "The general spoke so highly of you, I reckoned you to be more his age. Not that the general's all that old, mind you," he added hastily.

"I understand. The general and my father were close friends," Jessie explained without really knowing why. "I'll be looking forward to seeing him again."

"He's been summoned back to Washington, Jessie. Colonel McKenzie is in charge of Fort Butler. He's expecting

35

you. And about your horses, I'll see what we can do about getting them back."

"They took off that way." Ki pointed.

Stafford smiled. "Not by pursuit and capture, by ransom. Most things seized by the Indians can be bought back at a price."

"But that's blackmail."

"That's the way things get done around here," the lieutenant replied.

Fort Butler was more an assemblage of barracks and small buildings than an actual fort. There was no tall stockade so customary in other frontier posts. The post was more a division headquarters and Indian bureau agency than a stronghold of military might in a hostile territory. Most of the Indians in Indian Territory did not pose much of a threat. There was the occasional skirmish and the renegade bands that had to be dealt with, but rarely did the full force of the cavalry have to be brought against the Indians. At least not within the reservation lands. There were other fortified posts that carried on the active war with the Indians, but lately things in Indian Territory had been relatively peaceful.

Jessie was the first to comment on the untraditional look of the post. "This is not quite the picture I had of Fort Butler," she said as they entered the spacious military quadrangle.

Stafford, who rode alongside the wagon, smiled at Jessie. "I was a little let down myself. Fort Collins and Fort Cobb are probably more what you had in mind. They have a full stockade and the whole troop and their horses are garrisoned within the walls. But the Indians don't usually give us much trouble. We run a few patrols; it's mostly policing."

"You seem disappointed," Jessie said.

"I wanted to be stationed with the Seventh up in Wyoming."

Jessie gave him a strange look. "It's a good thing you weren't, or you wouldn't be here today."

"Oh, I don't mean for Little Big Horn. I was still at West Point when Custer had the command," he explained. "But there are still savages running wild, raiding and killing up north. Someone has to fight them."

"Not enough glory here for you?" Jessie said with a touch of bitterness.

"It's not glory, Jessie," Stafford began to explain. "I just want to do my part, an' help make this land safe for folks like you. But anyway, here we are."

Ki pulled the wagon in front of a large log cabin. The flag flew from a pole in the front yard, and a wooden shingle on the roof read, "U.S. Cavalry 11th Division."

They were announced, then ushered into the commander's office. Colonel McKenzie was a hardened veteran, with a thick gray mustache and heavy muttonchops. The cigar that dangled from the corner of his mouth looked to be a permanent fixture. As he sized up Jessie and Ki, he squinted in the manner of a man used to making decisions that control other people's lives. It was hard for Jessie to guess his exact age, but he looked old enough to make general and young enough still to enjoy it. One more campaign would probably earn him that star.

After proper introductions, the colonel got right down to business. "I don't know how much Major General Cropsey told you, but to be brief, homesteaders are being threatened by the Indians."

"But they may be settling illegally on Indian lands," Jessie argued. "In direct violation of the treaty we signed with the Comanches."

McKenzie ignored her and continued. "All in all we have the makings of an Indian uprising."

Jessie sighed heavily. "That's why we're here."

Again McKenzie squinted at them. "Yes, of course. What you can expect to accomplish is beyond me. Force is the only thing these savages understand."

"But force is the one thing that might provoke that uprising. To prevent another war, it seems the responsibility of the army to maintain the peace and make sure that—"

The colonel's deep voice cut her off. "Only the Indians can do that, Miss Starbuck. Treaties have been signed and it is up to the tribes to obey the law. It is not within our jurisdiction to prevent wars, Miss Starbuck, only to win them once hostilities break out."

"Not everyone sees it like that, though. It's also our responsibility to make sure that we uphold our side of the bargain. It takes both sides to keep the peace, Colonel."

McKenzie pointed his cigar at Jessie. "Let me tell you something. There is no peace with those savages. I've seen a chief sign a treaty on Monday and then his braves go and kill a family of settlers on Wednesday."

"It's about time we recognize the fact that one man doesn't speak for a whole Indian nation," Jessie stated plainly. "One chief can't sign a treaty for another tribe, and we can't hold him responsible for every Indian in a hundred square miles."

"My sergeant will show you to the Beckers'. I'm sure you'll all get along real fine." He turned back to his paperwork, then, as an afterthought, added his final words of advice. "But I will tell you this. The red man will always pose a threat to this great land of ours, and anyone who thinks differently is a damn fool!"

"The only good Indian is a dead Indian," Jessie said scornfully as she rose from her chair.

Colonel McKenzie nodded. "You quote General Sheriden. He's a great leader. He knows his Indians, and he knows from where he speaks."

"Just tell me one thing, Colonel. How many more Indians do you have to kill before you make general?" Jessie turned on her heels and walked out.

* * *

38

John and Lucy Becker were the friendly Quaker family in charge of Three Rivers Indian Reservation. Jessie took an immediate liking to the heavyset, cheery-faced woman. Lucy knew how to make one feel at home. Without any ifs, ands, or buts, she drew hot water for a bath and insisted that they would answer all their guests' questions after a hot, relaxing bath. After Jessie's run-in with the Comanches, and then her meeting with the equally abrasive Colonel McKenzie, a bit of relaxation was definitely in order.

After the bath and the change of clothes, they all had a more formal meeting in the main room, which served as the parlor and dining room. Jessie had many questions she was eager to ask. "The first thing I've been wondering," she began, "is where are the Indians? We saw more on the prairie than we have on the reservation."

John Becker was a tall, stern-looking man with short, sandy-brown hair. When he smiled, which was not often, his whole face became dominated by a long row of small but well-kept teeth. He smiled now at Jessie and Ki. "They're all camped over the ridge, about half a mile down by the river. When the cavalry moved onto the reservation, they picked up and moved, lock, stock, and barrel. They say they don't want to live within sight of the yellow stockings."

"Can't say I blame them," Ki muttered softly.

"Speaking of which, I hope thee didn't find Colonel McKenzie too disagreeable," John Becker said in a soft-spoken voice.

"It wasn't the best of meetings," Jessie said tactfully.

"He comes on with a bark that is much stronger than his bite. He is in charge of the military garrison, but he has no direct authority over how the reservation is run."

"He certainly didn't act that way."

"That is why Washington has seen fit to let us and my brethren administer the reservations. It requires a certain

39

patience and love for our fellow man, be they white or red. One must be able to turn the other cheek."

"But there is a fine line between being understanding and being abused," mentioned Ki.

John Becker nodded his head slowly. "That is the objection many have. When we first came here there were some incidents that thee may look upon as abuse." Lucy smiled briefly, but said nothing. "The Comanches would ride their horses through our home, and throw mud at our windows, but that is no more." Ki began to say something, then stopped as Becker continued speaking. "To answer thy question, Ki, there is a fine line when judgment is to be made, but we are not the ones to judge. There is only one capable of doing that, and in his eyes we are all his children, all equal."

"But there are too few people who see things that way," Jessie remarked. "Or we wouldn't be here now."

"Indeed. Unfortunately I don't know if thee can truly help, Jessie, but we are at our wit's end trying to avoid trouble that seems so imminent. From your expression I can see General Cropsey did not tell you much."

"No, he didn't. He said there was a problem at the reservation and you, and the Indians, needed our help."

"In a word, the problem is settlers. White settlers." Jessie and Ki exchanged glances. "The Indians have been treated poorly since they signed their peace treaty. Promises have been broken continuously, and conditions continue to worsen. And now that homesteaders are moving in on Indian land, there is talk of rebellion. Young braves threaten to go out on the warpath, and the army threatens to kill any Indian who acts the least bit aggressive. There have been too many killings; who knows where more violence will lead."

"I'm afraid it may lead to the massacre of the Comanches," Jessie said sorrowfully.

"Don't underestimate their warriors, Jessie," Ki interjected softly.

"But I'm afraid Jessie is right," Becker added knowingly. "There are enough soldiers here to wipe out the Comanches, though not before many settlers are killed."

"And if the Comanches are wiped out we'll have an even bigger problem on our hands," Jessie explained. "Three Rivers will become a symbol of the white man's treachery, a bad example of how we break our treaties. That could incite other Indians to leave their reservations." She paused to let her words sink in. "This one incident could be the spark that sets off a whole new Indian war."

Becker barely had time to ponder this point when there was an urgent banging at the door. Lucy excused herself and went to answer it. When they heard a high-pitched wailing, John rose and went to the door, with Jessie and Ki following close behind.

Just inside the door, a wretched-looking squaw held a woolen bundle to her chest. Her cries had diminished somewhat to an occasional sob. As Lucy coaxed the Indian woman into the kitchen Jessie realized the bundle she clutched to her chest was a baby wrapped up in a blanket.

Lucy took the baby and placed him on the table. It didn't take a doctor to realize the infant was seriously sick. His face was red and blotchy, and was extremely hot to the touch.

"Rubeola!" Jessie exclaimed. "Is there a doctor at the fort?"

"There is, but the Indians refuse to have anything to do with him. He's an army doctor, one of the yellow stockings who kill their people. They prefer their own medicine man."

"But the child could die. Surely she realizes that or she wouldn't have come here." Without hesitation she turned to Ki. "Find the doctor and tell him to come quick."

"Thee had better clear it with Colonel McKenzie first," Lucy suggested.

"Forget McKenzie," Jessie snapped. "Tell the doctor if he's not here on the double there'll be hell to pay with

41

General Cropsey." She turned to Lucy with a quick apology. "Pardon my language."

"Thee won't make a friend of the colonel that way, Jessie," Lucy said with a smile.

"This baby needs a doctor more than I need friends. Tell the woman her child is very sick but the white man's doctor will have medicine to help him get well."

"I understand your words," the Comanche woman said.

"Then you know I am a friend. I only try to help your baby."

The Indian nodded her head reluctantly. "Only a friend would care about my sadness, and only a friend would disobey Chief Yellow Stockings. Yes, I believe you are a friend to Yellow Deer and her child, but I do not know why."

"Because we are all sisters, Yellow Deer, and because your child knows nothing of hate and death. He doesn't know our people have been enemies, he doesn't know there are evil white men and evil Comanches. He only knows of the warm sun and the gentle breeze. And that is how it should be."

Yellow Deer said nothing, but nodded silently.

"Thee would make a fine Quaker, Jessie," Lucy said with much admiration.

The baby began to kick and cry, and the mother wrapped the blanket a little tighter around her son. "It's a good thing those blankets finally arrived," Lucy said to the Comanche. "We've been having trouble getting supplies, and with the cold weather coming we were all afraid there would not be enough blankets," Lucy explained to Jessie.

"Those blankets just arrived?" Jessie exclaimed.

"About a week ago."

"From where?"

"I don't know, Jessie. There are a few traders we deal with. Charlie Tyler is the Indian bureau agent, he would know."

"Why were you worried you wouldn't get the blankets?" The urgency in Jessie's tone flustered Lucy.

"Well, they said they didn't have enough blankets to go around. The reservations up in Dakota were hit by an early snow, and they were giving all they had to the Sioux."

"And then these just showed up?" Jessie asked. Lucy nodded her head. "From where?" Jessie persisted.

"Jessie, I don't know. When thee needs blankets thee does not look a gift horse in the mouth."

Jessie wasn't really listening, her mind was racing ahead. "How many children are there among the Indians?"

"It's hard to say . . ." Lucy began.

Jessie turned to Yellow Deer. "How many infants, little ones, are there among your people?"

"Fewer than the days of the moon."

"That means less than thirty," explained Lucy, "though how many less I can't say."

Jessie had a hunch, but she wanted to be sure. "These blankets, other mothers give them to their babies too?" she asked of Yellow Deer.

The Indian nodded. "The older ones have buffalo robes, they don't use white man's blankets. But the blankets, when they are . . ."

"Folded?" Jessie supplied the word from the hand gestures of the woman.

"Yes, when they are folded they are good for small ones," continued Yellow Deer.

Jessie shut her eyes momentarily, afraid of her own thoughts. "We may have enough," she said almost to herself. "We have to burn the blankets," she said very clearly. "All the new blankets must be burned."

"But why?" Lucy exclaimed.

"They may be infected with measles." She saw the look of disbelief on both woman's faces. "Where else would they get the blankets?" Jessie backtracked a minute to get them to follow. "If the agency ran out of blankets, where would they get more? Is it likely they would allot more money for the purchase of extra blankets?" It was a question that hardly needed answering. "But an unscrupulous trader can always get cheap blankets from a hospital. If they're used at all they're mostly used for livestock. . . ."

"But thee can not be certain these blankets are infected," protested Lucy.

"But can we be certain they're not? We can't afford to take that chance," Jessie said resolutely. She turned to Yellow Deer and explained the situation to her, but she could see she was getting nowhere with the Comanche woman. Horses, weapons, robes, and blankets were possessions of value to the Comanches. To ask them to burn blankets was like asking a white man to burn money. "There are two dozen blankets that Ki and I brought with us. They're out in our wagon."

"Why don't we wait and see what the doctor has to say?" Lucy said gently.

"I'll bring the wagon around," Jessie said firmly.

Later that night, Jessie awoke to a loud roar. The muslin curtains glowed a soft red. Wrapping the quilt around her body, she rushed to the window, where she saw the source of the light and sound. A large bonfire burned ten yards from the house. She dressed quickly and rushed outside.

There was really nothing to see. Even from the Beckers' spare bedroom she had known the fire must be made up of the pile of infected blankets, and by the time the blaze had reached the point where it woke her from her sleep, the Comanches who set it were long gone. But after seeing the blaze, Jessie was unable to go back to sleep. The heat from the flames was enough to fight back the cold of the night, but Jessie felt a chill inside her that would not fade no matter how close she stood to the roaring fire. The fire was not an empty gesture, it had its significance, and there was no doubt in Jessie's mind what it signified.

When the doctor had arrived he had only confirmed what they already knew. There was no mistaking the red blotchy skin and the high temperature. But he had

44

been hesitant to blame infected blankets for the one case of measles, though he did admit that the gestation period for the disease coincided with the arrival of the blankets. Only time would tell whether this was an isolated case of rubeola or the beginning of a larger outbreak. But now the wait was over. The pile of burning blankets was the answer.

Chapter 5

"Jessie, are you awake? There's a Lieutenant Stafford to see you." Lucy again tapped lightly on the door.

"Tell him I'll be right there," came Jessie's reply. She was lying on her bed fully dressed. When she had realized sleep was going to elude her she had gotten dressed, and had thought about walking up to the Comanche camp. But, she reasoned, most of the Indians would be asleep. Even if Yellow Deer were awake she would not know where to find her. One couldn't go knocking on every tepee in the middle of the night. So Jessie stayed in her bed and spent the better part of the night staring up at the ceiling, worrying about the sick Comanche children. There was nothing she could now do about her lack of sleep, but she ran a brush quickly through her soft copper hair. Jessie didn't know what the lieutenant wanted, but she didn't want to meet him looking like an old packmule.

As she stepped outside she was greeted by the smiling army officer. "Morning, Jessie. Thought you might like to take a morning ride." Stafford took a gracious but unnecessary step back; there was no hiding the two saddle horses that stood behind him.

"Our horses!" Jessie exclaimed with delight. "But how did you—" she began, then stopped abruptly, remembering what he had said the other day about ransomed goods. "How much do I owe you?"

"For what?" Stafford asked innocently, but his smile grew even broader.

"Two horses don't come cheap, Lieutenant."

"Are these your horses, Miss Starbuck?" Stafford asked with mock seriousness. He didn't wait for a reply. "I don't expect a woman to have to pay for her own animals."

"Stafford, I know how the Comanches prize horses, and I have a pretty good idea what an army lieutenant makes a month, so don't be acting foolish. I don't expect you to have to foot the bill."

Stafford remained unconvinced, but he did seem a bit embarrassed. "It wouldn't be a gift then, Jessie," he said softly. Then, adding a more businesslike tone to his voice, he continued, "If I'm interrupting your breakfast I can call again later.

"No, of course not," she said as she patted the neck of first the bay, then the sorrel. "We can leave right now. I'll run in and get my hat."

"It can get pretty cold out on the plain. Don't forget gloves."

"On second thought, Stafford, why don't you come in for a cup of coffee, then we'll leave."

Jessie wanted to ride up to the Indian camp, but Stafford suggested they follow the river south, and swing around to the camp on their way back. That seemed fine to Jessie. She had seen enough of the surrounding plains during their trip to the reservation, so they set off through the red cedars down to the riverbank. Jessie was soon glad they had taken the time for that cup of coffee. The open riverbed of the Big Moss created a natural wind channel, and even though the sun was shining brightly, there was a bitter sting to the wind. Soon the river forked off into two separate tributaries, and Jessie understood Stafford's selection of the route.

"This is where they got the name for the reservation," Stafford explained, "although technically it's probably only two distinct rivers. That's the Big Moss River, and it breaks off into the Little Moss and the Big Muddy." He pointed as he spoke. The Big Moss was deep and broad, and there was no indication how fast the water flowed till one looked at the narrower Little Moss and watched the water whirlpool around the exposed rocks that jutted out from the shallow water.

"I can see why they renamed it," Jessie said. "You'd never guess the Big Moss and the Little Moss were one and the same."

Stafford nodded and slid down from his saddle. "A few miles downriver the Big Muddy runs through a clay bed, but up here it's crystal clear." He walked to the water's edge and bent down to scoop up a handful. Jessie dismounted and walked beside him.

"It's beautiful."

"Someday it'll make a fine home for lots of folks," Stafford observed idly.

"It's already somebody's home," Jessie protested. She could see the puzzled look on Stafford's face. "The Comanches, or have you forgotten?"

"No, I haven't forgotten," he said with a touch of bitterness. Jessie didn't readily understand. "But this isn't their home. This is what we say is their home."

In a sense there was no arguing with his statement. The Comanches had once roamed over the whole Plains region from Nebraska to Mexico. And now they were confined to reservations. But Jessie couldn't figure out the slant to Stafford's ambiguous statement. "This was once all Indian land. We came into their home," Jessie said in an effort to feel him out.

The lieutenant shook his head. "They're nomads, Jessie. They follow the buffalo herds. They have no real home."

"We did a good job of getting rid of the buffalo, too."

Stafford nodded. "And one day I imagine the Indians will go the same route."

"I don't know why I expected something different from you."

Stafford looked genuinely hurt. "I didn't make the rules, Jessie. And I'm not responsible for progress. I didn't start it and I sure as hell can't stop it either."

"Then why don't you go up there with a few of your troops and just wipe them all out now? Just get it over with quickly." A slow smile crossed Stafford's face, but this time it held no charm for Jessie. "You'd like that, wouldn't you?" she said angrily.

"And don't you come off so damned innocent either. You own a spread that I'm sure some Indian tribe once called their own. And besides, you don't know what you're talking about."

That last comment rankled Jessie the most. "Because I'm a woman I don't know what I'm talking about?"

"No. Because you don't know the Indians like I do. I see them on a day-to-day basis, and I know they're just savages."

"You don't know everything, Lieutenant. You don't need to have red skin to be a savage," Jessie replied as she stomped back to her horse.

"But I do know that the Indians will never fit into the white man's society. And if they continue to live in the past they're doomed to become nothing more than history."

"Good day, Lieutenant," Jessie said as she swung up into the saddle and spurred her horse to a gallop.

Stafford hesitated a moment, then hopped on his horse. Jessie had a few seconds' head start, and her horse was running hard, but he had no doubts he would catch her. With a loud yell he took off in pursuit.

By the time he caught her, the hard riding had cleared away some of his anger. Though Jessie tried for a brief moment to outrun him, she quickly gave up the idea and slowed her horse to a walk.

"I owe you an apology, Jessie."

"You certainly do."

"No, not for what I've said. Like it or not, what I said stands."

It hit her suddenly. "You hate the Indians, don't you." She was so sure of it, it wasn't even a question.

"I got my reasons," Stafford answered curtly, in a serious tone. He lightened his voice, and forced a smile. "But that don't change nothing. I still owe you an apology—for something I didn't say."

"I think you've said quite enough already." Jessie was still annoyed. Not only by Stafford's attitude toward the Indians, but by the even more troubling fact that there was much truth to what he had said. She had stayed awake all night worrying about sick Comanche children, but now she had to face facts: more than just the lives of the children were threatened. Even under reservation law, there was so much friction and animosity between the red and white man that trouble seemed unavoidable. Even as she spoke she knew she was taking much of her frustrations out on Stafford. "You said too much when you asked me out for a ride. I don't know why you'd want to be with a know-nothing woman."

Again the lieutenant looked hurt. "Not because you know nothing, but maybe just because you *are* a woman. And a mighty pretty one at that. But I guess that was my mistake." He reined his horse around.

Jessie's words caught him quickly. "I believe you said you owed me an apology."

That brought a faint smile back to Stafford's lips. "I believe you think I paid money for your horses. Truth is they gave 'em to me for nothing. Yellow Deer is Running Wolf's squaw. It was a gift." Jessie began to laugh. "You're not mad?"

"I suppose I should be, but then you never said you bought them, did you?" Stafford broke into a huge grin, and for a minute Jessie wondered how she could have lost her temper with him.

"I was going to tell you right off, but when you made such a thing about paying for them, I didn't know what to say."

"Just say you'll ride up with me to the Indian camp so I can thank Running Wolf."

"Jessie, I'm sorry you an' me'll never see eye to eye. I'd best be heading back to the post. Just follow the river up, an' you'll come to the camp." He turned his horse and started back. This time Jessie didn't stop him. As she watched him go she realized something else. Lieutenant Stafford was afraid of the Indians.

Jessie found the Indian village with little trouble. The fifty or more Comanche tepees were set up in a loose circular fashion, and occupied most of the flat land between the river and two surrounding hills. It was an ideal location. Nestled along the west side of the river, the village had close access to water at a spot where the banks were high enough to prevent any flash flooding or high-water runoff during the wet spring months. The small rolling valley also offered a natural windbreak from the strong northern storms.

As she walked her horse through the village, Jessie felt very much the intruder. Although many women were doing chores outside their tents, no one said a word to her. She wanted very much to find Yellow Deer, inquire into the health of her baby, thank her for the return of the horses, and then be on her way. The village wasn't like any of the horror stories she had heard—specifically, there were no scalps hanging from any tepee flaps, or at least none that she saw. Still, she felt spooked, and realized the sooner she could leave the better she would feel. An elderly woman was tanning leather in the sun, and Jessie was about to ask her where she might find Running Wolf, when Yellow Deer stepped out of a tepee a few yards ahead.

Right off Jessie explained she could only stay a minute, there were other things to do, but she had wanted to stop by and see how things were. They had a pleasant but brief conversation. It was still too early to tell how her baby was doing, but four other children had come down with the measles. It was obvious from Yellow Deer's attitude that

51

she felt as uncomfortable playing host to Jessie as Jessie felt being her guest. Jessie didn't realize it at the time, but few white men, and practically no white women, had ever come up to the village. All transactions took place at the post, and all rations were given out there. Even when Jessie mentioned she had blankets to give to those Indians who had burned theirs, Yellow Dear said she would have the Indians come down and pick them up at the Becker house. Jessie told her that would be fine, then got on her horse and rode out.

She was relieved to get out of the village, but even as she headed up out of the valley the queasy feeling stayed with her. As she crested the ridge the feeling exploded into a full-scale nightmare. Everywhere she looked the plain was dotted with rotting animal carcasses. The dead cattle were in various stages of decomposition, and some looked to be only a few days old. She rode over to one of the fresher carcasses. She needed only a quick look. It was not that she was squeamish; she had faced similar sights more times than she liked to recall. Diseased cattle were nothing new to her. But there was an unease she felt at looking at so many, so close to the Indian village. Jessie turned away. Then the unease quickly ignited into anger, and she pushed her horse to a gallop.

"What are those cattle doing up by the reservation?" Though most of her anger had abated, and Jessie was able to ask John Becker the question in a reasonable tone of voice, there was still a trace of hostility to her words.

"Jessie, I'm not sure I understand," the man said, looking up from his desk.

"The plain's strewn with them! Carcasses everywhere. I've never seen so many in one place."

"Now please, Jessie, calm thyself."

It was good advice, and Jessie took a deep breath. "I'm sorry. I know I shouldn't be yelling. You're not the one responsible, but you are the one who can give me answers."

"It's their meat ration," he answered calmly. "They herd them up to the camp."

"No, you don't understand. I don't want to know why there are carcasses up there, I want to know why there are diseased carcasses."

John Becker looked even more confused. "They're bound to rot." It seemed obvious to him.

Jessie shook her head as she sat down. A dry smile crossed her face. "Anyone else might believe that. But you forget—I'm a cattle rancher myself. That's not just rot. Those were diseased cattle *before* they were slaughtered."

"I don't know anything about it. Maybe Charlie Tyler can shed some light on it. He's the agent for the Bureau of Indian Affairs." Jessie rose from the chair. "But he's not on the post. He left about two days ago, right after the last shipment of beef."

"A herd came through here two days ago?"

"With the army and Indian supplies."

"That's a start," she said almost to herself as she walked out of the office.

She practically knocked Ki over in the hall. "I was just going to start looking for you."

"And I was looking for you. I have something to show you."

"I don't think we have time, Ki. We have to hit the trail." She quickly explained the situation to him. "I want to find out who's selling diseased cattle, and how they get away with it," she said in summation.

"It might suit our purposes better to get a fresh start in the morning," Ki remarked.

Jessie thought a moment. "I guess you're right. And I could use a good night's sleep in a soft bed."

"Me, too," agreed Ki.

Jessie realized Ki was really saying it for her own benefit. Another night in the shelter in the warm house would do her good; Ki could sleep on a bed of nails. "All right. We won't lose much on a herd of cattle if we spend the night."

"Good, because I really could use the sleep," he said with almost a wink.

"Where were you all day? I didn't see you at breakfast."

"Same place I was all night. Come, I'll show you."

He took her out to the barn. There she saw the buckboard, filled with new blankets. "After last night, I figured you'd need some more blankets. From the size of the fire I'd say a good deal more. So I hitched up the wagon—"

"Where'd you get them?" Jessie seemed amazed.

"Stony Pond."

"But that's at least—" She stopped to try and calculate the miles.

"A good night's ride."

"And a good part of the day, too," Jessie added.

"I needed a town big enough to have blankets and a bank. I wired our bank for a draft." Ki had the look of a boy caught with his hand in the cookie jar. "I hope you're not mad."

"Mad?" Jessie exclaimed, then began to laugh. "I'm only mad for not thinking of it myself. I'm glad you did."

"I just hope I got enough."

"Don't worry," Jessie replied with a grin. "We can always send you back for more." Ki shook his head. "What's the matter, Ki, don't like the prospect of another all-night ride?" she chided some more.

"Oh, I don't mind that. But I cleaned the store out. There's not another blanket to be had at Stony Pond."

"I'm sure we'll have enough. Well, Ki, I think I'll turn in right after supper. I don't know about you, but I didn't sleep a wink all last night."

"Good, because I'll have the horses packed and saddled before dawn," he said with as big a grin as Jessie's.

Chapter 6

Even in the predawn darkness it wasn't hard to find the trail of the drover. It didn't take a skilled tracker—a couple hundred head of cattle leave a clearly marked sign. But it did take experience to tell the age of the trail.

"Well, what do you think, Ki?" Jessie asked.

"I'd say they passed through here not more than two days ago."

"Just checking. Becker didn't seem all too sure exactly when the herd left."

"If we ride hard today, we should catch them by the end of tomorrow. If they're not pushing too hard."

"If they have diseased cattle they won't be making great time. We might even catch them sooner. It looks like they're headed up the Chisholm Trail."

"Then they'll have to ford the Canadian River."

"Exactly. That'll be a day's work in itself. We should catch them on the other side."

"Not if we don't get started," Ki said playfully. He broke into a run, and Jessie took off after him.

That night Jessie didn't mind the hard ground and the cold air. She fell quickly to sleep. But she sensed more than heard Ki get up from his bedroll. "Lie still, there's something by the horses," came his whispered warning.

Jessie became instantly alert. She wondered if the intruders were Indians, but she didn't ask the question. Not only was there no way of telling, but any unnecessary sound might warn Ki's intended prey. What she did do was slip her hand around the peachwood handle of her Colt .38.

Ki padded silently to the horses, staying in a low crouch. He saw and heard nothing, but it was not his imagination. Both animals were untethered. He ducked under the horse's flank. There was a possibility that he had scared off the would-be horse thief. Silent as he was, he still might have been spotted in the hazy moonlight. But there was also the distinct, and deadly, possibility that somebody was out there waiting for him. There was enough cover in the thickets to hide a man in daylight. At night you could walk right up to the brush and not know someone was lurking there till the barrel of a shotgun poked against your ribs. Ki slipped a *shuriken* between his thumb and forefinger. With a sinking feeling he realized there might be more than one man concealed in the bushes, so he slid another silver throwing star into his palm.

Ki now had two options. He could remain where he was and wait for his hidden adversary to make the first move. Or he could try to outflank him, and come upon the bushes from behind. If the man—or men—had not seen Ki either plan would work. But if Ki had been spotted, there could be a gun trained on him at this very moment. The next move of the horse, no matter how slight, might open up a clear shot. Ki was not prepared to gamble his life on whether or not he had been noticed.

Life was never a sure thing, there were no certainties. Gamble and risk were always involved, especially in the life of a warrior, but Ki had spent a good part of his life training to limit his risk in any given combat. The trick was to accentuate your strengths and cover your weakness. It meant understanding and playing the odds. And right now, Ki didn't like the odds. So he changed them.

He burst out from the cover of the horse, throwing himself headlong into the grass. There was nothing subtle about his move, nor was there intended to be. He planned to do two things. He hoped to draw the fire of his hidden adversary, and he hoped to avoid getting shot. When he hit the ground and heard the first shot go off, he accomplished his first task, and as he rose to his knees two rolls later he realized he had accomplished his second task. He spun around quickly and let the *shuriken* fly in the direction of the shot. He was about to let loose with his second throwing star when he heard the sound of a horse in flight.

It was a good thing Ki had not tried to outflank the gunman. In one respect he had miscalculated the situation. The gunman was not hiding in the bushes ahead of him, but almost directly behind him. Had he tried to surprise the man, or even wait by the horses, he would have been a sitting target. Ki raced to his horse to take chase, then stopped. The man was also farther back than he had expected him to be, or he would not have gotten to his horse so quickly. That meant he was already on his way out as Ki had sneaked up on him. Ki cursed himself silently and raced back to the campsite. Jessie's bedroll was empty.

Ki would have continued to berate himself for his stupidity if there had been time, but there wasn't. Obviously the noise by the horses had been a ploy, a diversion to get Ki away from Jessie. It had worked, and now Jessie was abducted into the night. Ki had to get his bearings. The man who had shot at Ki had fled to the northwest. Would Jessie's kidnappers have gone in the same direction, or would they have used the other rider as a decoy, and headed off by a different route? He would make that decision when the time came, but right now he still had a few seconds' grace before he would be mounted and ready to go.

He jerked his horse to the northwest and crashed through the thickets. He had not gone more than ten yards when he saw the glint of moonlight reflect off the steel barrel of the gun. He drew his animal up short. "Jessie!" he exclaimed.

"Ki, I thought you were—" Jessie began with a mixture of shock and relief.

"I thought *you* were—" Ki said, equally excited.

"When I heard the shot I came running."

"When I saw you were gone I thought . . ."

Jessie began to laugh. "It's a good thing I didn't shoot you."

"It's a good thing I didn't trample you."

"We're just two lucky folks," she said with a smile.

With the danger gone, and Jessie safe, Ki's emotions calmed and his practical side returned. "There are still many hours to daybreak, enough for you to get a good night's rest."

"And you?"

"I'll keep watch."

"I don't think he'll return. It was probably just some drifter thinking to steal an easy horse," Jessie reasoned. "Why don't we both try to get some sleep?"

"All right," Ki agreed. "I'll sleep lightly."

They crawled back into their bedrolls, but Jessie had a feeling Ki would remain awake the rest of the night.

The next morning Ki remained unusually silent as they continued to track the herd. Jessie turned to him playfully. "Don't be so glum, Ki. You can't hit every time."

"What was that, Jessie?"

"I said, not every throwing star is going to find its mark. After all, it was dark, and you were spinning around behind you."

Ki cracked a smile. "I didn't miss. This morning I went back to look through the thicket. I didn't find my *shuriken*."

"One lost *shuriken* doesn't a bullseye make," Jessie teased.

"There was blood on the ground," Ki stated plainly. "A hit, but a nonlethal one."

"You don't know that. Why, right now some poor horse thief may be lying face down in the dirt cursing your Japanese ancestry with his last breath."

"I don't think so."

"Then if you didn't miss, and you don't have some dead drifter on your conscience, why are you so glum-looking?" Jessie persisted.

"Last night I feared you had been abducted."

"But I wasn't," Jessie said brightly.

"But for all my vigilance you could have been. I made a sloppy, foolish mistake. This time I was lucky."

"You mean *I* was lucky."

Ki laughed. "Yes, you were lucky. And I was lucky too." His smile broadened. "We're just two lucky folks," he said in a playful mockery of Jessie's comment the night before.

"Then cheer up."

"But I feared you were abducted," Ki repeated, his tone once again serious.

"Honestly, Ki, sometimes I just don't understand you." That returned the smile to Ki's lips. "And you find that funny!" Jessie continued in exasperation.

"No, Jessie. You see, I felt you were in some terrible danger, and I don't think a common drifter or horse thief would leave me with such trepidations."

"I wouldn't worry about it, Ki." She didn't have time to explain why before the first shots rang out.

Jessie pressed low against her horse's mane and bolted for the nearest cover, a shallow gully a few yards off to their right. There might have been the possibility of outrunning the gunfire, but that was not the Starbuck way. If someone was shooting at Jessie she wanted to know who and why. Sticking behind the cover of the horse, she slid quickly to the ground, pulled her Colt from its holster, then whacked the animal's haunch. In the slight depression she would be protected, but the horse would be exposed to any stray shots. It was important to keep their horses alive; on foot they would be truly at the mercy of their ambushers. Ki slid down right next to Jessie, also sending his horse trotting off into the distance.

"Our friend from last night?" asked Jessie.

"Friends. Sounds like there are two."

Jessie nodded. "A very interesting pair. They've gone from horse thieving to bushwhacking. Let's make sure they don't progress to murder." She began firing her pistol. There was no way of seeing her target; she didn't even raise her head out of the gully. But right now that wasn't the objective. Their foe was out there somewhere, and the only indication as to where was the sounds of their gunfire. As Jessie pumped the Colt, her fire was returned. After a few rounds she stopped and turned to Ki. "Well?"

"Two, all right. Over in that dry wash. One behind the cottonwood, the other I think in the gully to the left. They're amateurs."

"How do you figure that?" Jessie asked.

"They don't have high-powered rifles, and they were lying in wait too far from the trail. Trained assassins would have concealed themselves closer and caught us in a cross-fire."

"I'd hate to be shot dead by professionals," Jessie said dryly.

Ki ignored her sarcasm. "That means we have the advantage."

"What do you propose?"

"I'll run out and draw their fire, and you nail 'em."

"How quaintly put," observed Jessie. "What if they were pros?"

"I'd run out and draw their fire, and you'd nail 'em," he said with a smile.

"What if I miss?"

"You won't."

"What if they don't expose themselves?" Jessie persisted.

"Then we'll think of something else."

"But you'll be out there right in the middle of their sights."

"I'll make sure not to stay in them too long," Ki assured her lightly.

Jessie didn't appreciate his humor. That he wasn't really joking bothered her even more. "Why can't we try to surround them? You go left, I'll go right."

Ki shook his head. "There's no cover out there. We'd be hit before we made ten yards."

"Ki, I know you're right. But there has to be a better way than sending you out there."

"We could just sit here. Maybe they'll get bored and leave."

"Why don't we try to get the horses and hightail it out of here?"

Ki shook his head again. "Jessie, I want to know *why* those men are shooting at us. Besides, we'd never make it to the horses."

"Then what makes you think you can dodge their bullets?"

"Nothing. But I'm willing to try." Jessie was about to speak again when Ki cut off her protests. "I don't think I can dodge their bullets forever, but then, I won't have to, will I?" he said cunningly.

"I don't like it, but we'll try it."

"Good. Go for the one behind the tree first. I'll try to keep the other one down. Now relax."

Jessie nodded her head and took a deep breath. She told herself it wasn't really as dangerous as it seemed. She was quite capable of knocking out the ace of hearts at this distance, and she knew it, but a playing card would not be shooting at her friend. She took another deep breath and steadied herself. She had always been a good shot, and with Ki's instruction she had become exceptional. She would calm herself and focus all her concentration on the tree. Nothing else would exist but the gunsight, her finger, the trigger, and the tree. Her bullet would find the first

61

thing that moved. She had no doubts whatsoever. She turned to Ki and nodded. "I'm ready."

"Jessie, one other thing. I wouldn't want to go out there without being totally honest."

"Okay," Jessie said softly.

"They know we're one man and one woman. I don't think they'll be expecting you to know how to handle a gun very well. I'm not taking all that much of a chance."

"Because I'm a woman!" Jessie exclaimed angrily. Ki shrugged and gave her an innocent smile. She returned the smile. "Why Ki," she began sweetly, "I do believe you're trying to rile me up."

Ki edged over to the far end of the gully and rocked gently on his heels. He spoke softly to himself and Jessie, "One, two, three . . ." Suddenly he sprang out like a jackrabbit. He ran low to the ground, zigzagging back and forth. Bullets hit the dirt all around him, but neither Jessie nor Ki noticed.

On three Jessie aimed her gun and waited. It seemed an eternity, but was scarcely more than a second. A pale spot of pink stuck out from behind the tree, and Jessie squeezed the trigger gently.

Ki had been listening intently for that one gunshot. When he heard Jessie fire he dropped to the ground. As he lay there the air became very still. He had known it would not take Jessie more than one shot. As the sniper had stuck his head out from behind the tree to take aim, Jessie had dropped him.

Ki had hoped the man in the wash would not notice what was happening and would eventually reveal himself to Jessie's sights as well. The other gunman, though, had caught on quickly. He saw through the trick and now hugged the cool sand of the dry wash. All three of them were pinned down, afraid to expose themselves for fear of catching lead. It was almost comical, Ki thought to himself. If it weren't so deadly, he might have laughed out loud. There was one chance to pull out of this successfully, but it depended again on Jessie.

Jessie saw the sniper drop, and immediately turned her attention to the other gunman, but out of the corner of her eye she saw Ki drop too. Fear gripped her soul. She was terrified to believe what she saw. Ki had to be all right, he just had to be. Slowly she got control over her thoughts. What was she really seeing? She hadn't seen Ki get shot. She just saw him lying facedown in the dirt. But what did she expect? That he would run all the way to the wash and pull the gunman out by his collar? Rationally, she knew Ki had probably dropped deliberately, but then, was it rational that Ki could dodge all those bullets without one lucky slug hitting him? Whether he was wounded or not, he was still trapped right out in the open. She realized there was only one thing for ther to do. Softly she whistled for her horse.

Ki continued to lie facedown, not moving a muscle. Any movement, no matter how slight, could end with a slug of lead. The minutes ticked by. Then he heard it, the sound of the horse's hooves. A smile came to his face. He didn't turn around to investigate the sound; instead he waited patiently. He didn't have to wait long. In the next instant the gunman stood up from the wash and aimed his rifle. At the sound of the shots, Ki pumped three bullets into him.

Jessie reared her horse around and came to a thundering stop alongside Ki. "You had me worried back there for a minute. I thought maybe you had gotten hit."

"That's probably what he was thinking, too," Ki said as he gestured to the dead body.

"I figured if I made a run for it, he would assume you were dead and would try to get me before I got too far."

"How did you know he wouldn't?"

Jessie's face stretched into a smile. For a minute she didn't answer, then she said, "The same way you knew they wouldn't hit you." Ki chuckled at that. "If it was good enough to work once, I reckoned it'd work again."

Ki turned his attention to the body that lay at his feet. "So much for gaining any information," he said almost to himself.

"Three bullets, my, my. How unlike you, Ki." Jessie couldn't be certain, but she thought she saw him blush ever so slightly at her teasing words.

"I didn't want to take any chances," Ki said simply.

"Thank you, Ki."

Even though both men were dead, and carried no identifying papers, Jessie and Ki were still able to determine something of their origin. They were covered with dust, their boots had fresh manure on the soles, and they wore dirty bandannas around their necks. It was Jessie's guess they were working the cattle herd. They found the cowboys' horses, and slung the bodies over the animals' backs. While Ki lashed them securely in place, Jessie rounded up his horse.

As Ki climbed up into the saddle he turned to Jessie. "Just one thing. How did you know I wasn't really shot?"

"Because you're awfully good at playing possum," she said playfully. Then she thought a moment. "I think if you were really dead, I'd know it for certain."

Ki didn't say a word. He felt the same way about Jessie.

Chapter 7

They caught up with the herd on the near side of the Canadian River. It was late afternoon, and the fact that the herd had not crossed the river spoke much of the incompetency of the trail boss. The herd would lose another day crossing the river, whereas if they had pushed across this afternoon they would be well rested and ready to go by morning. In Jessie's mind incompetency and dishonesty went hand in hand. But as they moved down to the chuckwagon, she saw few, if any, diseased cattle among the couple hundred head.

They raised a few eyebrows, but no one said anything to them till they came to a stop. A husky man, wearing a long leather jacket and dark Stetson, moved through the handful of trail hands. "Can I help you two?"

"We're looking for the trail boss," Jessie said flatly.

"You found him." The stub of his cigar remained firmly situated in the corner of his mouth, but when his eyes went to their two packhorses, he pulled the stogie from his mouth. He had a hard, deeply lined face that showed little emotion.

"You know these two?" It was only a rhetorical question; it was obvious he did.

"'Knew' seems more to the point. Jake Smith and Ned Jones, two of my hands." Jessie raised an eyebrow at such obvious aliases. The trail boss read her thoughts. "Don't matter what they call 'emselves, s'long as they can rope an' ride. Where'd ya find 'em?"

"Can we talk in private, Mr. . . . ?"

"Brunner. William Brunner." For the first time he gave a close look to Jessie and Ki, his eyes narrowing slightly as he focused on the Japanese-American. "We can take a walk behind the wagon."

Jessie dismounted and followed Brunner. "What outfit you with?"

"The Double R, out of Texas," Brunner said proudly.

"I don't place the name," Jessie thought out loud.

"It's my own brand. I have a small spread at the headwaters of the Red River."

Jessie nodded. She couldn't know every rancher in Texas. Just because she never heard of Brunner's Double R didn't make him a criminal. That he hired gunmen and sold diseased cattle to the Indians might, though.

Brunner interrupted her thoughts. "So where'd you find 'em?" he asked with concern. "Though I don't have much sympathy for hands that quit in the middle of a drive," he added quickly.

"We came upon them on the trail. They were lying in wait for us."

Brunner had no doubt about her meaning, but his eyes showed surprise. "I wouldn't have figured them for bushwhackers. They kept to themselves, but they handled a rope as good as any."

"Good thing they didn't handle a gun as good," Jessie said without any humor. "But that's not why I wanted to talk to you alone." Jessie studied the rancher. Brunner seemed guarded, but not openly hostile. She decided to plunge in headlong. "I want to know why you're selling diseased cattle to the Indians. I know a little something about ranching, so you'd best give it to me straight."

"I wouldn't be so modest, Miss Starbuck," he said with

a smile. "And I wouldn't try to snow you," he added sincerely.

"How did you know my name?"

"You're somewhat of a legend among Texas ranchers, an' I just put one 'n one together. Your Oriental sidekick, your knowledge of cattle, and"—he hesitated briefly—"your good looks."

"That's not quite two," Jessie said curtly. Her tone did not ruffle Brunner.

"I reckon if I was a better counter, I'd make a better rancher. But I didn't mean you no offense, ma'am."

"Now about the cattle?" Jessie persisted.

"That's in the contract. Not exactly in words, but they ain't paying top dollar, they don't want good beef."

"Who's this 'they'?"

He was surprised by the question. "The Bureau of Indian Affairs, the Department of the Interior. The people who run the agency and the fort."

Jessie thought it over for a minute. Brunner took her silence as a sign of disapproval. "Miss Starbuck, I don't make the contracts, I just deliver my side of the agreement. There's always gonna be a few head that get sick, you know that, and there ain't nothing wrong with the beef either, and if they don't make the arrangements with me, they get another rancher to deliver sickly cattle, simple as that."

Jessie knew there was truth in what he said, but that didn't make her like it any. Even on her own trail drives, Gimpy would butcher sick cattle and feed the meat to the men. But only certain cuts, selected with care, could be used. The cattle sold to the Indians were not butchered skillfully. Jessie commented on the abundance of dead and discarded carcasses around the Indian village.

Brunner shrugged. "The contract calls for meat on the hoof. That's what they get."

"You supply the army as well?"

"Yeah. They pay per cut pound."

Someone like John Becker would not realize what that really meant but to Jessie the whole picture became clear. The army was buying top-grade meat, and paying the going rate; to supply the Indians anything was good enough. But it was even worse than that. Meat on the hoof meant just that. The animal was weighed and the price set. That the buyer was paying for bones, hooves, and heads always meant more money per animal, but the price balanced out by not paying slaughtering fees. What would make this look acceptable on paper but disgusting in practice was that with diseased cattle there was very little usable meat per head. But a good price was still commanded.

"Who writes your contracts? Who's the buying agent?" Jessie knew better than to blame the low rung on the ladder.

"Charlie Tyler."

She had found out what she wanted to know and turned to leave. Brunner stopped her. "You and your man are welcome to stay for supper and bed down for the night."

Jessie knew that many small ranchers had to get by any way they could, and she couldn't hold Brunner personally responsible for the situation. Like he said, if his Double R didn't fill the contract some other rancher would. Still, she looked at him with contempt.

"I'm lucky to have the trade," Brunner explained. It wasn't difficult to read the thoughts behind her scornful look. Jessie continued to scowl, thinking of the sick and hungry Comanche children. His tone changed to one of apology. "I know it ain't fair," he began softly, "but then it weren't fair when the Comanches stole my little girl."

Jessie and Ki stayed the night. In the morning, Brunner asked if Jessie and Ki would like to hire on. He was shorthanded, and if they were going the same way, he could use two more hands. He would be happy to pay them a more than fair wage. Jessie apologized. She really would have liked to help the man, but there were more pressing matters

68

back at the reservation. But she did promise to wire ahead and have two cowboys meet Brunner farther up the trail. With a "much obliged" and an invitation to his Double R spread any time they were in the neighborhood, Brunner waved them good-bye.

Jessie was in a foul mood for most of the morning. After a few miles of silence she turned to Ki. "I never thought there'd be anything I'd ever like about the cartel," Jessie said with a bitter smile.

"And what's that?"

"They were rotten to the core. No doubt about it, everything they touched stank."

"Let me guess. Brunner is not the lying cheat you had envisioned."

Jessie nodded. "Two wrongs don't make a right. But that's only a small part of it."

"It's not so black and white any more."

"That's what I mean. With the cartel you always knew where you stood."

"There's still a right and a wrong here, Jessie. We just have to root it out."

Jessie shook her head. "Brunner, the Caldwells, and the Beckers all mean well. I think in the end everyone is going to lose."

Ki disagreed. "I don't think *everyone* will lose." There was an ominous tone to his voice.

Jessie understood. "I guess if we don't do something, the Indians will suffer the most. But what do we do, Ki?"

Ki remained silent. His answer bothered her for the rest of the day.

They stopped late in the afternoon. A stiff wind had sprung up, and the temperature was dropping quickly. When they came upon a small, semisheltered grove of cypress trees, they decided to make camp. There was an abundant supply of wood, and the ground held more buffalo grass than rock. They wouldn't find a better site.

They had just finished their simple but satisfying dinner

of beans, biscuits, and dried beef, when Ki sniffed at the air. He got up and walked around the fire to stand upwind. He sniffed again. "I smell woodsmoke," he remarked cautiously.

The sky was just beginning to darken, and Jessie searched for a sign of light on the barren prairie. "I don't see any signs of a fire."

"Neither do I," agreed Ki. "I'd better have a look." They both knew it was possible to build a fire that would not be noticed by others.

"I think I'll come with you. I want to see who it is that's building a fire he doesn't want others to notice."

"Let's not jump to any conclusions, Jessie. They might have camped in a small gully, or the fire might just be embers."

"You're right, Ki. There could be lots of reasons why we don't see any reflection of the fire. There could also be one very good reason." Jessie picked up her holster and strapped the Colt .38 around her shapely waist.

Ki nodded, then sniffed at the air again. "Let's leave the horses here and walk. It can't be too far."

The night air was full of the aroma of the prairie: the subtle smells one could not always place, the delicate fragrances that were always changing. Each season had its own blend, each wind held a hint of something that came from beyond. It was one of the things Jessie loved about the land, and one of the things she missed most when she was away. It amazed her that in the large cities this smell of sage and mesquite was all but gone, and few people would ever miss it. As they walked silently over the short patches of grass, she realized this land was home for many. She wasn't only thinking of the Caldwells and other white settlers, she was thinking of the animals that had roamed this land long before any white man's eyes laid sight on them. The buffalo were of course the most obvious, but there were also elk and white-tailed deer, as well as the smaller mammals and rodents: coyotes, bobcats, rabbits, possums, and prairie dogs. The land also supported wild turkeys, quails, and migrating geese. Even though Jessie spent a good part of her life out in the open, she never took it for granted. She was not always consciously aware of her feelings; sometimes a mountain was just something to get over, a river something to ford, or a prairie to ride across. Her day-to-day business would often encroach, but it never blocked out the fact that Jessie deeply loved this land that was her home. At that thought, a wry smile came to Jessie's face. This land was also home to the Indians.

As much as she or other settlers would come to love this land, she doubted any would ever respect it like the Indians. A settler might love the land for what he could get out of it; an Indian revered the land for the part he was allowed to play in it.

Ki put out a warning hand and pulled Jessie from her reflections. He pointed to his ear, and Jessie listened closely. Faintly, she could hear the crackling of burning wood. They were close. Close enough for the horses to pick up their scents. There came a slight whinny. Jessie reached down to her holster and silently eased the Colt out. The element of surprise was now lost. As they moved closer, the horse let out another cry. From beyond a row of straggly shrubs they heard a thick voice.

"Quiet! I can't shoot every damned coyote just 'cause they give you the jitters." The speaker was a portly man, probably in his late forties. At least he seemed to be portly. Wrapped in blankets the way he was, it was hard to tell. There was also very little light. There was a fire, but it burned from the bottom of a deep and narrow pit. That explained why they had not seen the flames or their reflection against the rising smoke. It also said that here was a man who wished his presence to go unnoticed.

Jessie and Ki observed the man silently from behind the bushes. He was traveling alone, by wagon, and didn't seem to pose any threat, at least not in the condition he was in. The man hummed softly to himself as he kept sipping

71

from a tin cup. Jessie didn't have to see the bottle that rested against his leg to know the man was drunk.

Jessie stood up and entered the clearing. "Howdy," she said loudly.

The man jumped and reached for the shotgun that lay by his side. Ki leaped into the air, his foot making contact and knocking the weapon away before it was even leveled. "Oh, now, why'd y'have to do a thang like that for?" There was true remorse in his words. As Ki landed, his rear foot had knocked over the bottle of liquor. "I got me plenty more, but still I don't like to waste none."

"We don't like having shotguns pointed at us," Jessie explained coolly.

The man laughed and tipped his hat. "That there's just meant for the Injuns, ma'am. Y'gotta watch yerself out here."

"Is that why you built a pit fire?" Ki questioned.

"Can't be too sure, friend. Better safe than sorry."

"Have any trouble with Indians lately?" Jessie inquired.

The man eyed her cautiously, then shook his head. "Naw, I try and stay clear of 'em."

"That just might be a tad difficult, seeing as how you're in Indian land right now."

"Don't intend bein' here long. I'm just a poor peddler passin' through. Can I ease either of your thirsts?" he said as he held up the bottle.

"We were stopped by a party of braves the other day. They were looking for whiskey," Jessie said casually. "You'd best be careful."

"It's a big place. There's plenty o' room for the Comanche, Kiowa, and Stopher Dineen."

"How did you know this was Comanche land?"

"I make it my business to know such things. And it's common knowledge, ain't it?"

Something in his demeanor made Jessie very suspicious. It didn't seem likely a man wary enough to build a fire in a pit would then get drunk with hostile Indians possibly lurking in the area. Ki was also suspicious, for as Jessie talked to the man, he slipped off to have a look at his wagon.

"What exactly do you sell, Mr. Dineen?"

"You ask a lot of questions, ma'am."

"Pardon me, it's part of my nature."

"And it's part of my business to be cautious, you'll understand," he answered with a smile. "Dr. Dineen's magic elixirs, tonics, and ointments. Refreshers, revitalizers, and rejuvenators," his voice ticked off in singsong fashion. Jessie was just beginning to accept the man on face value —he did seem like a typical drummer—when Ki called out to her.

"Jessie, I think you'd better come have a look at this."

Jessie walked over to the wagon. Ki had pulled back its tarpaulin cover. There were six large wooden barrels, and many cases of unmarked quart bottles. Jessie picked one up and uncorked the stopper. She didn't need to taste the liquid to guess just what Dr. Dineen's magic elixirs were. The smell gave it away. In the Kentucky hills they called it moonshine. Many Indians called it firewarer. Running Wolf called it crazy water. Jessie simply called it rotgut. To the Indians it was a deadly poison, and it was illegal on any Indian reservation. She turned to Dineen. "This is prohibited on Indian lands," she began, but stopped abruptly when she saw the man had a Colt .44 drawn and leveled. She also noticed that he held it with a remarkably steady hand.

Chapter 8

The gun never wavered; it pointed unerringly at Jessie's chest. Dineen's eyes never moved from his target, but his voice addressed Ki. "Don't try any of your funny stuff," he warned. "I'd hate to put any unnecessary holes in the young lady. Though I don't have much of a likin' for low-down trail thieves."

"We're not thieves," Jessie stated plainly. She was amazed how quickly his thick, drunken voice had cleared.

"No, you don't look like your average bushwhackers," he mused, "but these days, who can figure?"

Ki eyed the man carefully. He was unsure of the peddler's intentions. It was possible Dineen was only protecting his goods and meant them no harm. But Ki never relaxed when a gun was aimed at Jessie. "Accidents" could always happen. As long as the threat remained, Ki thought of nothing but removing the object of that threat, whether it was man, beast, or weapon. He watched the man, looking for an opening. There was too much distance to cover with a flying kick, so Ki waited for the man's vigilance to drop. The moment Dineen's concentration slipped or the gun moved off its target, Ki would be on him. As long as Jessie kept him talking Ki figured he had time. It was when men stopped talking, when they had made up their minds and come to conclusions, that bullets started flying.

"And you don't look like a cold-blooded killer. Or are looks deceiving, Mr. Dineen?" Jessie said caustically.

"No, I'm no murderer."

"You're certainly no simple peddler either. Smuggling whiskey to the Indians is a serious offense."

Dineen let out a hearty laugh. "It's always refreshing to come upon somebody who genuinely cares."

"I don't find that particularly funny."

"No? Well, that's what makes a horse race."

The smuggler paused for thought. Jessie felt the same urgent need to keep the man talking. "I still don't see what's funny about caring for the welfare of the Indians," she persisted.

"It's fine and dandy to care about the savages, now that they're all prisoners on reservations. But you didn't hear much concern for them when they were raiding settlements. . . ."

"The hostilities are over, Mr. Dineen. We're all trying to live together now," Jessie said softly, hoping not to inflame her captor.

Again Dineen let out a laugh. "You don't understand, but few really do. It works both ways, miss. I ain't condemning the savages. But then I don't go around proselytizing about the plight of our poor red brother either."

Jessie felt stung by the insult. "My concern is greater than—" she began, but was cut off.

"Where was all your concern when Sheridan trapped Lone Wolf, and Custer massacred Black Kettle? Sometimes I do believe that poor Stopher Dineen is the only one who cares about our savage brethren."

"How?" Jessie asked angrily. "By killing them with your whiskey?"

Dineen shook his head. "By offering them a way to ease their pain and suffering."

"It does more than that, Mr. Dineen. It makes them downright crazy."

"Moving them from their homelands makes them crazy.

Putting them on reservations makes them crazy. Making them live in a white man's world makes them crazy."

"They can learn to live in our world," Jessie reasoned out loud, though she wasn't quite convinced of it herself. "If we give them a fair chance they can."

"But with men like you that's just about impossible."

"For a woman of sense and reason you do have a way of surprising me. No, miss, I wouldn't place all the blame on me, or men of my kind. We're just cogs in a wheel."

"But you're part of the problem."

"I simply supply the Indians a choice. I give them the good and the bad of the white man's civilization."

"And that wagon is an example of the bad." Jessie was getting fed up with the smuggler's self-righteous behavior.

"I'm not so sure about that. Drink has brought out the best in many a man, and relieved the dreadful pain in many a tortured soul."

"You might just as well shoot them all and put them out of their misery. Which I imagine you'll do to us just as soon as you've finished proving your virtue."

"You've brought up a very interesting problem. Like I said, I ain't a murderer, but you understand I just can't let you go. Least not yet I can't." Keeping the gun trained on target, he moved over to the wagon. From underneath the seat he pulled out a coil of rope, and tossed it over to Jessie. "Tie his hands and make sure they're tight," he ordered.

"I've never been too good with a rope," Jessie said demurely.

"I think you'll learn right quick," the smuggler said as he pulled back the hammer of his Colt. He directed his voice to Ki: "Get yer hands behind yer back."

Jessie stepped behind Ki, and Ki did as he was ordered. "Make sure they're tight, Jessie. I think our friend means business."

"Now I sure hope you didn't mean anythin' funny by

76

that, friend. 'Cause if yer hands ain't tight, you won't be usin' them ever agin.'"

Dineen's words sent a cold shiver through Jessie. But there was no call for the threat. Knowing Ki, Jessie took his words at face value. It was not like the man, in any situation, to say anything but what he meant. Behind his back, Ki placed his wrists one over the other. She bound them together firmly but allowed his fingers to move freely. Jessie thought she understood. If Ki could reach one of his *shurikens,* in time he could slice through the ropes. It didn't matter how tightly his wrists were bound.

Suddenly Ki let out a little groan of pain. "I think that's plenty tight, Jessie. Any tighter and I'll be losing circulation." His complaint confused Jessie. Why would Ki attract attention to his bonds if he planned to slowly cut his way free? As she finished binding Ki's hands, she felt his fingers reach out and grab hold of hers. She took a small step toward him, and he took a firm hold on her arm. She looked up, and proclaimed simply, "Done."

"We'll just have a look now, and see what a good job you done," Dineen said with a smile. Nobody was going to put one over on him. He moved closer. On his second step Jessie felt Ki's weight press backward against her. Suddenly she found herself falling to the ground, Ki's body on top of hers. She hit hard and had the air knocked out of her. When she regained her breath it was all over.

Ki had known if he could close the distance between himself and the smuggler he wouldn't really need the use of his hands. He had been confident he could knock the man out with one or two well-placed kicks. But Ki wouldn't try anything as long as there was any risk to Jessie. He had formulated his plan quickly the moment Jessie stepped behind him to tie his wrists.

It had been simple to goad the man closer. Ki stood directly between the smuggler and Jessie. She was safely out of the line of fire. Even if Dineen managed to get a shot off, Ki's body now protected her. Still, Ki wanted to be absolutely certain. A swift push on her arm and a little body weight had sent Jessie sprawling to the ground.

The moment he had felt Jessie start to lose her balance, Ki's left leg had shot up and out, catching Dineen's gun-hand right at the wrist. The gun had gone off, but the momentum of Ki's kick sent the man's hand waving high into the air. The bullet whizzed by safely overhead. Ki had noted grimly that the gun remained in the tight grip of his assailant. But in truth it mattered little. Almost immediately after his left leg connected with Dineen's hand, Ki's right foot hit its mark, coming up hard under the man's chin. First the base of Ki's heel had dug hard into the man's Adam's apple. Dineen's eyes bulged slightly as he gasped for air. Then the powerful snap of Ki's muscular leg had actually lifted the smuggler up off his feet. When Dineen landed on his back, Ki could see he wouldn't be getting up right away; the man was out cold.

Ki turned to Jessie, who lay on the ground behind him. "Sorry about that, Jessie," he said ruefully. "I hope you're okay."

Jessie got shakily to her feet and brushed herself off. "I'm doing a lot better than he is." She gestured to the prostrate Stopher Dineen.

"Don't worry, he's not dead," Ki informed her.

"I wasn't," Jessie replied evenly. "But what happened? I thought you were planning to cut through the ropes with one of your *shurikens*." She suddenly remembered that Ki's hands were still tied behind his back and went to free him.

"That would have been one way, but it would have taken time. Who knows what he would have done? There was a better way." As Jessie stood behind Ki untying the ropes she realized what he meant. Ki continued. "But I'm sorry I had to fall against you."

That was typical of Ki, thought Jessie. He had saved them from danger, but was now apologizing for whatever inconvenience he might have caused her. Even more than that, he had risked his own life by using his body as a shield for her. She wanted to say something that would express her gratitude, but couldn't seem to find the right words. She knew that whatever she said, Ki would downplay his courageousness in his usual modest way. He would simply point to the unconscious Dineen and deny that there ever had been much of a risk.

"Throwing myself against you gave me greater leverage and leg extension," Ki continued to explain.

"Glad I could be of some assistance, Ki," Jessie teased good-naturedly.

"You do tie a mean knot, Jessie," Ki remarked with equal good humor as he rubbed his wrists.

"I think Mr. Dineen is about to find that out as well," she said as she crossed over to the unconscious smuggler. "But I don't know how pleased he'll be by that. When he wakes up he'll find himself standing on the wrong side of the fence."

This time the Comanches seemed to materialize out of nowhere. They had come upon the wagon silently and swiftly, the way an autumn storm creeps from a cloudless sky. As there was no chance to fight or flee, Jessie simply pulled back on the reins and brought the wagon to a stop. Stopher Dineen, trussed up in the back of the wagon, cried out in pain as his sore head banged into the sideboard. "Ma'am, please, my head."

"We have bigger problems than your hangover, Dineen," Jessie snapped, though she knew the source of his pain was not an excess of alcohol. "Some of your customers are paying a visit, and I don't think it's going to be a happy one." She ignored his further questions and turned to Ki. "Do you think they'll believe the truth?"

"What else could they believe?"

"If I were an Indian I'd think it a little suspicious myself," Jessie concluded. But there was no more tine to talk.

The first Comanche rider pulled alongside the wagon. *"Tesha,"* he said with a smile.

Jessie returned the smile. "Yes, Running Wolf, friend."

"Then why do you lead a wagonful of white man's poison? What need have you for this crazy water?" There was no need for the Indians to search the wagon, it was obvious what the cargo was.

"It is not ours, Running Wolf. It belongs to this man. We are taking the man and the wagon back to the fort."

The Comanche leader poked at the smuggler with his lance. "Why?"

"He is a dangerous man and a criminal."

Running Wolf smiled slowly. "I do not wonder why you have a man such as this bound like a pig. I wonder why you take him back to the fort?"

The whiskey runner had the prudence to remain silent, but his eyes more than shouted out his fear. Jessie took only one quick look at him before turning to the Indian to answer. "You know the army forbids the sale of whiskey to the Indians. He has broken the law and must be punished," Jessie explained.

"Justice." Running Wolf's single utterance was not a question, but it showed little understanding for the meaning of the word.

Jessie wasn't sure if the Comanche meant something by his ambiguous statement, or if he was just practicing his English. Still, she nodded her head anyway. "Yes, justice."

"White man's justice." Running Wolf spat out the words, and now there was no misinterpreting his original meaning. It was obvious the Comanche had little faith that a white man would be punished by a white man for doing harm to the Indians.

"He broke the law, and he will be punished," Jessie repeated.

"A trial?" Running Wolf asked.

"There will be a trial."

"I wish one buffalo still roamed the plains for each

white man who has walked free from a trial of justice," Running Wolf said humorlessly.

Inwardly, Jessie smiled at the Indian's sophisticated understanding of the white man's legal proceedings. She herself had bristled many times over when a fancy, high-priced defense attorney had fast-talked or bought freedom for his guilty clients. But she was too worried about Dineen's safety to be amused for more than an instant. Much as she disliked the man and his actions, whiskey running did not seem like a hanging offense to her, and she didn't want to see Dineen put to death at the point of an Indian lance. There was also another angle to be considered, and she did not hesitate to speak her mind. "If you kill him, Running Wolf, you will have broken the white man's laws. You will be treated as a murderer and then you will be brought to justice in the white man's court."

"There is no justice for the Comanche. Your courts have no justice for any Indian."

Jessie realized she had taken the wrong tack and tried again. "If you kill a white man, the yellow stockings will hunt you down."

"I am not afraid to see that justice is done. I am not afraid to be hunted."

"But it will go bad for all your people. If just one reservation Indian kills a white man, your whole village will suffer." Jessie could see the Indian thinking it over.

Running Wolf began to speak slowly, as if he were thinking aloud. "What you say is true. But that is only if the yellow stockings find out. If there is no one to tell of the murder, they will never know."

Now it was Jessie's turn to realize that what the Indian spoke had much truth to it as well. By trying to save the worthless whiskey smuggler, had she unknowingly sealed her own fate, and that of Ki's as well? If all three of them were to die out here on the prairie, who would be the wiser?

"But we are friends," began Running Wolf. A slow

smile crept over his face. "There would be no peace in my tepee, when my woman learns I have let harm come to those we call friends." In Comanche, he barked out an order to the other braves. Immediately, one went to unhitch the wagon horse while another untied Jessie and Ki's horses from the rear of the wagon.

Jessie had the distinct feeling she had been through this once before. This time she didn't bother elaborating on the rights of ownership, or the lack of merit in horse-thieving. She simply resigned herself to the simple fact that the horses were not meant to be hers. It would mean a long walk back to the fort, but at least their lives were no longer in danger. There was a relief to that, but Jessie still felt bitter, and refused to sit by and say nothing. "I hope you enjoy them, Running Wolf," she said sharply.

As the Comanche turned to her, there was pain in his eyes. "Only the white man gives gifts and takes them away." The brave came up and handed Jessie the reins to her horses. "You take him and go." The Comanche pointed to Dineen. "The wagon stays here."

Jessie started to protest, but Running Wolf cut her off. "Go now, before I change my mind."

Ki carried Dineen to one of the saddle horses and helped him get set for the ride. Meanwhile, Jessie went over to the unhitched wagon horse and tied the long reins shorter. She then grabbed the gray mare around her mane and swung easily up onto her bare back.

Jessie's grace impressed the Indians, and Running Wolf decided maybe he had been too abrupt with his friends. "If you ride the wagon to the fort, maybe he will find justice, maybe he will not. That is of little importance. But somehow, someday, this poison"—he pointed to the wagon—"will surely find its way into the stomachs of many of my people. That can not be allowed. Now go."

They didn't have to be told twice. The three whites urged their mounts forward and didn't look back till a half-mile later, when they heard a sudden roar. Turning in her

82

saddle, Jessie saw the burning wagon. It must have taken the Indians that long to uncork or smash all the bottles and kegs of liquor. As she watched the blaze, one of the wood casks burst into flames, sending balls of blue fire shooting high up into the sky.

The American flag was just being lowered as Jessie, Ki, and Dineen pulled up to the division headquarters. "I hope the colonel is still in," Jessie said as she swung down from the gray mare's back.

She entered the building and was in luck. Whatever Colonel McKenzie was, he at least put in an honest day's work. He looked up from his desk and seemed neither pleased nor annoyed to see Jessie standing in front of him. "I was just leaving for the day, Miss Starbuck."

"This won't take long. We caught a whiskey smuggler."

The colonel's interest showed. "How many Injuns you bring in?"

"We have the smuggler," Jessie repeated, a little more emphatically. "It *is* against the law to sell whiskey on the reservation, isn't it, Colonel?"

"It's also against the rules for the Indians to buy or consume liquor. How many kegs did he have?"

"A wagonload," Jessie replied.

With a heavy sigh the colonel stood up from his chair and grabbed his hat. "Let's go have a look at the contraband."

"The wagon was destroyed by Running Wolf."

McKenzie looked at her shrewdly. "You're saying you have a smuggler, but you have no proof."

"There's my word, and Ki's," Jessie said belligerently.

"I can't arrest a man to suit your whim, Miss Starbuck." His voice softened and became very placating. "What's to stop anyone from waltzing in here and accusing anyone they don't like of being a thief or a smuggler?"

"I'm not just anyone, Colonel McKenzie." The challenge in her voice was clear.

The officer retreated somewhat. "Let's have a look at the man. But even if I arrest him, without proper evidence he doesn't stand much of a chance of being convicted."

"Whose side are you on, Colonel?"

"I'm not on anybody's side, Miss Starbuck. I'm an officer in the United States Cavalry." He stepped out the door, then turned back to her. "And from here on in, please leave enforcement of the rules and regulations to the army."

Outside, a respectable distance from Ki and Dineen, a small circle of Indians had formed. Among them Jessie picked out Running Wolf. Apparently they had come to see if justice would be served, but they also had the very obvious side effect of making Stopher Dineen quite nervous.

McKenzie seemed oblivious of the Indians' presence. He took a quick look at Dineen, then ordered his sergeant to cut the smuggler's bonds. "This woman has accused you of smuggling whiskey onto an Indian reservation." Dineen remained silent. "Do you deny the charges?"

The smuggler took a long look at the Indians who stood ready and waiting. It was possible that with the right answer the colonel might allow him to walk free, but even Dineen questioned the wisdom behind that. Earlier, the Indians made it clear what their intentions were; only Jessie's intercession on his behalf had spared his life. He could save himself from arrest, but there were many miles till the reservation border. "I'm not saying anything till I see a lawyer," he said prudently.

"Very well. Sergeant, take this man to the stockade. And see to it that these Indians are dispersed." Without even a glance at Jessie the colonel turned and walked off.

As the sergeant took Dineen by the arm the smuggler turned and faced Jessie. "This may seem like an odd time to say this, ma'am, but I'm much obliged to you." A smile crossed his face as he looked down at the sergeant's tight grip around his arm. "For back there, that is," he added to clear any doubts.

Jessie acknowledged him with a nod of her head. Even to herself she didn't want to admit liking the pompous, self-righteous smuggler. She turned to Ki. "Now let's go see that Indian bureau agent." As they walked to Tyler's office she noticed that the Indians had all disappeared as quickly and quietly as they had come.

The agent's office was dark. Jessie called out to see if the man was in back preparing supper, but after a few tries they both decided no one was home. It was time to head back to the Beckers' and call it a day. They attended to the horses, then hunkered down to a well-cooked meal, compliments of Lucy Becker.

As Jessie washed the supper dishes—Lucy had put up a valiant protest, but Jessie wouldn't have it any other way —something started to jell in her mind. "Ki, something's bothering me," she said as she handed a plate to Ki.

"You want me to wash and you'll dry?"

"About Dr. Dineen." She was not in a jovial mood.

"You don't think he'll be convicted."

"I don't know, but that's not it."

"You're wondering how a man can be likable yet commit evil," suggested Ki.

"That's part of it. How does he strike you, Ki?" she asked, but did not wait for his answer. "He's a friendly, amiable huckster, and a drunk."

"And . . .?" prompted Ki.

"And I'm not sure what I'm trying to say, Ki, but something doesn't fit."

"I think you're still looking for the cartel, Jessie."

Jessie stared down at the soapy dish in her hands, then turned to him excitedly. "That's it, Ki. That's what's missing," she exclaimed.

"I almost wish it were that simple this time," Ki said under his breath.

"No, listen," she said enthusiastically. "No matter what

their scheme, the cartel always liked to use pawns to do their dirty work. Some were innocent and others not so. But whether they knew it or not, they always did the cartel's bidding and fit right into the plan. And I look at Dineen and I can tell he's a pawn, as is that drover Brunner."

"Now, Jessie, I wouldn't be screaming conspiracy everywhere I look."

"But it all fits together so well. They're all using the Indians, all taking advantage of them."

"Jessie, that's part of the situation here. Greedy, dishonest white men are all too ready and willing to prey on the Indian. There's nothing new about that."

"But in this case it's all working to provoke a deadly confrontation," Jessie said earnestly.

"But to whose benefit?" Ki wondered aloud.

"When we find that out, we know who to go after. And I think our Dr. Dineen can give us a few clues."

First thing in the morning, Jessie marched over to the stockade. At first the guard refused to let her see the prisoner, but after throwing around a little muscle and dropping the name of General Cropsey, she soon convinced the soldier it was in his best interests to let her in. She had to find out what Dineen knew. Getting the information from the smuggler was too important to let any obstacle bar her way. Nothing would stop her. That was, until she stepped into the jail.

"Oh, my God," Jessie exclaimed softly.

There, hanging from the bars of the window, his neck in an improvised yet very effective noose, hung Dr. Stopher Dineen. His feet dangled only inches above the floor, but it was enough. Jessie would never get the answers to her questions. And Dr. Dineen would smuggle no more whiskey, sell no more rejuvenating tonics, tell no more tales . . . ever.

Chapter 9

"I just don't believe it could be suicide, Ki." Jessie and Ki walked along the ridge behind the Beckers' house. Not only was she too upset to sit still, she also wanted to have unencumbered privacy to discuss even the wildest theories of what could possibly have happened.

"Maybe it wasn't," Ki answered. "Maybe Running Wolf changed his mind."

Jessie shook her head. "If he wanted to kill Dineen I think he would have done it right out on the plains, when he first had the chance."

"Maybe it wasn't Running Wolf, but another Co-manche. There could certainly have been others who wanted to see the man dead." Jessie listened attentively. "It could have been possible to lure him to the window from the outside, then wrap the belt around his neck."

"His own belt?"

"You have a point," conceded Ki.

"I even thought that someone could have slipped past the guard, but McKenzie vouches that no one could have. The guards were stationed at their posts all night."

"It doesn't seem likely that Dineen would kill himself. He didn't seem the type," agreed Ki.

"And I had a feeling he knew that without the whiskey as evidence there wasn't much of a case against him."

"Yet you found him dead."

"Well, suppose—just suppose—that there *is* someone instigating trouble here. Isn't it possible that whoever hired or supplied the whiskey to Dineen would realize just what I realized?"

"Which is?"

"That as long as Dineen lived he might spill the beans. To insure his own safety this person would have to make sure that no one could expose him."

"But Colonel McKenzie said no one could have made it past the guards." There was no reason for Ki to say more. He realized the full implication of his thought almost immediately. Yet Jessie could see doubt on his face.

"Well, why not, Ki? The cartel corrupted men even more powerful and influential than Colonel McKenzie. Why shouldn't personal greed and ambition do the same?"

Ki knew it was true. "But what would he gain?" he asked nonetheless.

It only took a moment of thought to come up with the answer. "Glory."

"It's a persuasive spirit," Ki agreed.

"If hostilities were to break out, McKenzie could send in his troops and wipe out the Comanches. It would be a feather in his cap, and probably earn him a promotion to general. And at his age there can't be too many chances left."

Ki nodded in agreement. "The fierce Comanches. It would put his name right next to Custer's and Sherman's."

"It will, unless we can stop him," Jessie said resolutely.

"What do you propose?"

Jessie shrugged. "The usual?" she asked with a grin.

Ki looked puzzled. "The usual? There is no usual."

"Right. We just stick our heads into every hole till we get it bit off or come up with the snake between our teeth."

"Right," Ki said flatly.

"Don't complain," Jessie said with a grin. "It's worked up till now, hasn't it?"

"With a few close calls." Ki needn't mention the many last-minute rescues he had to pull to save Jessie from the jaws of the cartel.

Jessie seemed unfazed. "Close only counts with horseshoes and scatterguns," she pronounced.

They turned and started to walk to the fort. Jessie still had things to discuss with the agent for the Indian bureau, Charlie Tyler. There were a lot of unanswered questions, and he might be able to shed some light on those hazy areas. Jessie walked with a bright step. She was confident that with enough poking around they would come up with enough rope to hogtie Colonel McKenzie.

Ki, though, was not so confident. Often problems did have simple solutions, and even the most complicated situations could be broken down to simpler parts, but it seemed almost too easy to put the blame on the one man who wielded the most power. With each development the situation on the reservation exposed layer upon layer. Too many layers, Ki felt, to pin everything on the most obvious man.

"Something doesn't fit into your theory, Jessie," Ki puzzled aloud.

"I don't have all the answers, Ki, but at least we know where to start looking."

"Often that prevents the discovery of the real solution."

Jessie smiled. She understood what Ki was saying. "I kept an open mind, but now it's staring us in the face. Who else could be in a position to instigate an Indian uprising and then benefit from the putting down of that uprising?"

"McKenzie may not be the only one to benefit," reasoned Ki.

"But he was the one who said no one could have gotten past the guards. That was his mistake."

"But, Jessie, if he wanted to instigate trouble, he could have pinned the murder on a Comanche, rather than pretend it was suicide. That would have given him due call to

89

arrest a handful of Comanches and then who knows what kind of trouble would erupt."

"Maybe his pride kept him from doing that. It wouldn't look good for a savage to have gotten past his soldiers. But maybe you're right. Maybe that was his first mistake."

Ki thought a moment. "Unless, of course, it was no mistake at all. Maybe it was a warning."

Jessie looked hard at Ki. Her voice firm and resolute, she said, "Then that was his *real* mistake. We don't scare off." There was no boast to her words, just simple fact. They walked a moment in silence, then, "And I think I'll tell him just that," Jessie added menacingly.

Ki never got to finish voicing his objections to Jessie's theory; they had already reached their destination. Until Ki could figure out some of the missing pieces, he would keep his opinion to himself.

"I think I'll stop in and have a word with McKenzie before we go see Tyler," Jessie said as she turned to the division headquarters.

They were about two hundred yards from the building when a buckboard went racing past them to pull up in a quick stop in front of the headquarters. The driver dumped a large bundle onto the ground: from the distance Jessie couldn't be certain, but it looked like a body. The driver pulled out his revolver, took aim at the lump, and fired twice.

Jessie and Ki broke out into a run, but by the time they got there soldiers were already crowding around. Jessie pushed her way up to the front. On the ground, facedown, lay a dead Indian. She turned to the closest soldier. "Quick, go get the doctor," she ordered.

"It's a little late for that, ma'am."

Jessie turned to study the Indian and realized it was true. All the color had drained from the Indian's face, and there was a dark pool of congealed blood over his heart. The Indian was dead long before the last two cartridges were pumped into him. She saw Lieutenant Stafford in the crowd and hurried over to him. "What happened?" she asked.

"That fellow Partridge found this Indian trespassing on his land."

"And . . . ? Simply trespassing doesn't get a man killed. Even an Indian," she added dryly.

"When you're butchering someone else's hog it does."

"Oh." She studied Partridge. There was nothing unique about him, yet he seemed to be cut from a different cloth than other homesteaders, such as Sam Caldwell. Perhaps it was the slant of his Stetson, or his ever-moving, dark beady eyes. Jessie refrained from asking further questions; Colonel McKenzie had just stepped out of the building.

Partridge was seated in his wagon, reins in hand, when he saw the colonel. "I got plenty more cartridges, Colonel. You tell those thievin' Injuns you're protectin' that any more of 'em come 'round my place, and they'll wind up jus' the same." With that warning he whipped the team forward.

"I want this Indian taken up to the village, now," commanded the colonel, then he turned and stepped back inside.

Jessie was astounded. "He can't just let that man ride away," she protested. Stafford didn't seem very concerned. "He murdered that Indian."

"Not everyone would see it that way, Jessie," Stafford started to explain.

"This has gone too far," Jessie exclaimed angrily.

"Take it easy, Jessie." Ki had come up alongside them. "It would be like arresting a man for shooting a horse thief."

"But we only have Partridge's word for what happened."

"Around here that's enough," the lieutenant informed her.

Jessie was still mad, but she realized there was nothing she could do, especially for the slain Comanche. She turned to Ki and moved onward. "What did you think of Partridge?"

"I'd say he wore his revolver a bit low for an honest homesteader."

Jessie agreed. "I think he looked more like a cartel plug-ugly than a farmer, too. And I think I know who might have some information about Partridge."

"Jessie, I never got around to finishing what I started to say on the way over here. There's one fly in the ointment. Someone might be instigating trouble, but the main source of the problem is the homesteaders. Families like the Caldwells. I don't see how McKenzie can fit into that."

Jessie nodded thoughtfully. She didn't have an answer, but Ki's comment brought to mind another problem. "Someone better go out and warn the homesteaders. There might be trouble."

"Indian reprisals?" said the lieutenant, though it was not really a question.

Jessie thought of the small room and the acrid gunsmoke that had quickly filled the Caldwell home. "I wouldn't want Sam Caldwell to be caught unprepared."

"Someone also better get up to the Comanche camp," Ki suggested.

Jessie quickly recalled the uncomfortable feeling she had the last time she was up at the Indian village, but she knew that if someone didn't go up and try to talk sense to the Comanches, the whole powder keg could explode right now. Jessie looked at Stafford, then Ki. "Someone who is sympathetic to the Indians," she said pointedly, "but someone they'll also respect."

"I don't think a woman's voice will bear much weight in a council of war, Jessie," Ki said sympathetically.

Jessie seemingly ignored Ki's comment and continued. "Someone who has proven himself worthy. . . ."

"Someone who has the spirit of the tiger in him," Ki concluded with a smile.

"Would you, Ki?"

He nodded. "I don't know how successful I'll be."

"Ki, if they give McKenzie even the slightest cause, he won't hesitate to march his soldiers right through their village."

"I'll try my best."

"Good. And I'll start out to the Caldwells."

Ki turned and walked off. Stafford waited for him to get out of earshot, then addressed Jessie. "I'm sure the colonel will be dispatching men to the various homesteads. If you'd like I could escort you to the Caldwells."

"All right."

"Let me just clear it with him. I'll be right out."

Lieutenant Stafford returned a few minutes later. He did not seem pleased. "The colonel is sending out parties of three. He doesn't want to take any chances. And he specifically doesn't want you out riding the reservation."

Jessie wasn't about to let the colonel restrict her movements, but she was disappointed over losing Stafford's company.

The lieutenant misinterpreted her displeasure. "Personally, I think he's a little afraid that General Cropsey'd have his hide if anything happened to you." Jessie doubted that but said nothing. "For myself, I just regret the loss of your company." A slow smile crossed his face. "But then again, if I were to just find you out on the trail tomorrow morning . . ."

"You couldn't just let a lady go along unescorted," Jessie finished with a smile. "At least not with hostiles possibly lurking nearby." As soon as she said it she regretted it. Depending upon Ki's success or failure, what seemed like a joke today could be the threatening, deadly reality of tomorrow.

As Ki walked through the Indian village many women silently watched. He noticed there were no braves to be seen, but that did not surprise him. The dead Comanche had already been brought up to the village, and Ki imagined all the men were in a powwow. He was not sure if he would readily be invited into their council, but he continued to walk steadily toward the center of the village, where he assumed one of the larger tents held the gathering. As he moved closer, the sound of heated voices soon disclosed the site of the meeting. Ki was unsure of the proper protocol. How did one get to voice an opinion, especially if not a member of the tribe?

He turned to a squaw who stood outside a nearby tent, and called out to her in a clear, even voice. "Pardon me, ma'am. Could you tell me where I might find Running Wolf?" He felt foolish speaking to her that way. She probably did not understand English, and even if she did, would probably not answer him. But getting an answer was not his intention. He was hoping his voice would be heard by those inside the tepee, and that someone, preferably Running Wolf, would step outside. Ki was not disappointed.

"I come as a friend, to address the council."

Running Wolf looked at him shrewdly. "There is nothing for you to say to us. Though you are only a halfbreed, you still speak the white man's lies."

"You are wrong, Running Wolf. I do not come to speak lies. I come to tell you things that the white leaders do not wish your people to know."

Though the Comanche seemed curious he remained firm. "We know enough. We know that the white men who steal our land now kill our braves. That is enough."

"No, there is more. There is trickery and deceit. Your people will only suffer more if you do not listen."

Before Running Wolf could respond, a thick gravelly voice called out from the tepee. Running Wolf turned and responded in his native tongue. After a short exchange, of which Ki understood nothing, Running Wolf turned back to Ki. "Black Elk wishes to see you," he said as he held the tepee flap open for Ki.

Ki stepped inside and was immediately impressed by the

spaciousness of the tepee. Although there were many braves, sitting three deep, there was no feeling of being cramped or confined. In the center of the tepee was a small fire pit. The smoke rose to the opening in the top of the tent, heating the tepee without filling it with smoke. It was the first time Ki had been in an Indian tepee, and he would have liked to study it more, but the aged figure who sat directly opposite him demanded his attention. Ki bowed serenely. "I am honored, Black Elk," he said with much reverence.

Black Elk was the peace chief of the Comanches. In all the matters not concerning war, he would have the final, and sometimes only, say. His word was to be regarded as law. His face was deeply lined, and his eyes, though old, still had a bright, alert spark to them. A single row of eagle feathers sat atop his still-lustrous long black hair. Black Elk lifted the ornate fan of gray and white eagle feathers that he held in his lap and indicated for Ki to sit. "I welcome you, Spirit HalfBreed. *Numinu* have few friends. Speak your mind." His words were slow, but his voice carried the weight of authority.

"*Numinu*," Ki began, using the native term for Comanche, "are a proud people. I do not wish to see them tricked by the white man. I do not want to see them doing bad deeds to benefit the white man." He proceeded to tell them briefly of his suspicions that the Indians were being goaded into taking hostile action. He also outlined the repercussions these actions would precipitate. He concluded with his belief that Colonel McKenzie only waited for the opportunity to ride his soldiers through the Comanche village. "When they come they will come with guns blazing and swords slashing. They will not distinguish between warriors or woman, young braves or little children," he warned. To his surprise there was no reaction in the tepee to Ki's dramatic words. Did they doubt his sincerity; did they not believe the soldiers would attack? As the silence grew and became absorbed in the thick hides of the tepee wall, Ki wondered if all his efforts were in vain.

Finally Black Elk spoke. There was a sad smile on his face. "You speak from the heart, Spirit HalfBreed. But your words make no difference."

"As sure as the sun rises in the sky, the yellow stockings will swoop down upon your village and kill your people," Ki said earnestly. "You must believe that."

"We are familiar with the white man's ways," Black Elk said painfully.

It bothered Ki that Black Elk associated all white people with the evil individuals he had encountered. But he understood. From the Indian's point of view there were probably very few white men who did not break their promises or do the Indians harm. Still, Ki had to impress upon the chief that Jessie and he were deeply concerned with their plight, and that they could actually help the Comanches. But in his heart Ki wondered if there really was anything that he, Jessie, or, for that matter, anyone else could do to help the plight of the Indians. Sometimes things went too far to be held in check. The force of a rushing river could not be diverted as it crashed over the waterfall. Whether for good or bad, sometimes events had to play themselves out to their conclusion, even if it were to a deadly ending. This might be the Indian's destiny. But as Ki sat before them he realized that he was now also entwined in that destiny. He had a role to play. He could not walk away from that, and not because he had told Jessie he would do his best, but because he chose not to. He found he truly cared for the Comanche people.

He brought his thoughts back to the matter at hand. "Not all white men wish you harm. Jessica Starbuck, myself—"

"That may be," interrupted Black Elk, "but the white men with the guns all think alike. The yellow stockings have raided many a peaceful Indian village. They have slaughtered many women and children. I have seen this

96

myself." There was much sadness in his voice. "It is not that we doubt your word, Spirit HalfBreed. But it matters little."

"But for the sake of your people," Ki protested.

"The white men already kill my people. They destroy the buffalo, which give us our food and our homes. They imprison us on our own lands."

It struck Ki how accurately the whiskey smuggler had summarized the Indians' plight. "But what is done is done, Black Elk. You can not change that. But there are still decisions to make that will greatly affect your people."

"I have heard you are brave, Spirit HalfBreed; now I see you are also wise. But you will never understand. You are not one of us. The river winds its way through the earth, that can not be changed. The waters still flow and still bring to us the white man's hatred. Season after season, my people roam their lands, our children are born, they grow and then in turn have children. We live and prosper. But now the white man comes and our children die of blotched faces."

Ki understood what the elder Comanche was getting at, and wanted to change the topic. "But your brave who was just killed was murdered. Let Jessie and me find the man who is responsible. He will be punished." Ki looked to Running Wolf and thought about the whiskey smuggler. "Running Wolf knows I will do as I say."

Black Elk shook his head. "One brave matters little." His hand reached out and squeezed at the air dramatically. "But as our children die our people slowly die as well." His old withered hand seemed to tighten around the neck of an imaginary foe.

Ki could well imagine the power that was once in those hands, and the strength that still remained in the chief's soul. He realized then that Dineen was wrong in one respect. The Comanches could be lied to, cheated, and even murdered, but their spirit would never be destroyed. He knew his time in council had come to an end. He rose and bowed, then turned and stepped out into the cold air.

Chapter 10

Ki had not realized how long he had sat in the Indian pow-wow. He was used to long, meditative sessions, and his legs would not cramp, regardless of how long he sat in one position. But the sun had still been high in the sky when he walked into the Comanche village, and now as he walked back, the landscape was a flat shade of gray. The sun had already set, and the first stars were starting to twinkle faintly in the cloudless twilight sky. He walked slowly back to the Beckers. He wondered what he would tell Jessie; had he even accomplished anything?

As he pondered that question, he thought he heard a faint sound behind him. It was probably the wind, nothing more. But as Ki listened, the soft sound came again, too regular to be the wind. More on instinct than anything else he whirled around quickly. There behind him stood one of the largest Indians he had ever seen.

The man looked like a typical Comanche brave. He had the broad face, dark eyes, and muscular body, but everything was on a larger dimension. He was taller, broader, and heavier than his companions. Standing by himself it was hard to realize that he must have towered over his fellow braves. Ki widened his stance and readied himself.

"I come as a friend." The Indian had the deep booming voice one would imagine coming from such a barrel chest.

"You walk quietly, as an enemy," Ki remarked.

"I did not wish the others to know I had followed you. Can you find those who killed Little Knife? Can you see to it they are punished?"

"I think so," Ki replied.

"I think if you do that, they will be pleased. I think there will be no trouble, if the white murderers pay for their crime."

Ki eyed him curiously. "Why do you feel this when Black Elk speaks differently?"

"We are a proud people, Spirit HalfBreed. But no one wants to bring death upon themselves. If we find the murderers there will be no trouble."

"We . . . ?" Ki questioned curiously.

The Comanche nodded his large head. "It will bring me great honor to help capture these white men. I know where Little Knife was shot. I can take you there."

"If you know who these men are, why do you come to me?"

"I do not know who the men are. I only know where Little Knife was going. And I know he did not return. I could go with other braves, we could kill the men we think did it, but that would not help. We need you to bring these men to the white man's justice."

"You will take me to where you think Little Knife was killed?" The Comanche nodded. "But no one else knows you do this?"

Again the Comanche nodded. "Stalking Bear listens to his own heart. There is no one else who will think I do right. But I do what must be."

"I understand. Tomorrow I will meet you at sunrise."

Stalking Bear hesitated. "It is some distance away. We should leave tonight. The night is still young. There will be a bright moon. We can travel much before we sleep."

The Indian seemed nervous and ill at ease. Perhaps he feared he would change his mind if they had to wait till morning, and Ki did not want to lose this opportunity. It mattered little to Ki if they left now or at sunup. "I will get my horse now."

"Good." Stalking Bear pointed to the west. "I will meet you on the trail, at the forked tree," he said, then turned and slipped away silently.

They rode for a good many hours before Stalking Bear brought his big roan to a halt. Ki looked around cautiously. Stalking Bear had been nervous and uneasy the whole ride. He sat casually in his saddle, but even in the dark Ki could see the Indian's neck muscles tighten at every sound. He had assumed that Stalking Bear was just nervous of being caught by his fellow Comanches, but now as Stalking Bear stopped, Ki thought the Indian might have heard something. Somebody could be out there. Ki pulled his bay alongside Stalking Bear and noticed the Comanche did not look on his guard; in fact, he seemed more relaxed now than ever.

"We will rest the horses now," Stalking Bear announced, then slid down from his mount. "We have come far enough from the village."

Ki thought that was an odd way of marking distance. Was Stalking Bear that worried about being discovered, or was it simply a different style of communicating? "How much farther to the spot where Little Knife was killed?" Ki asked his guide.

The Comanche looked thoughtful. "By morning," was his simple answer. He pointed to a skin pouch hanging from his saddle. "There is water here."

Ki nodded. He knew enough of Comanche ways to know that the water was not intended for himself, but rather for the horse. Comanches were notorious for their ability to ride the plains for days with little or no food or water. Their horses could sometimes withstand the same rigors, but the Indians respected their animals enough not to put them through any unnecessary hardships. Similarly

Ki wondered if they were stopping to take a rest or if the stop was only for the horses' sake. He decided to ask.

"We can eat and rest and get warm. You can sleep if you want, only a short time. We should keep moving."

"Why the hurry, Stalking Bear?"

"I want to be back in the village before they know I am gone," he answered without hesitation.

If Ki suspected treachery he would not have expected the Indian to give him such a frank reply, yet he could not understand the great need to be so secretive. If Ki managed to bring in Little Knife's killers, then Stalking Bear would quickly step forth to accept the praise of his people. If, on the other hand, they returned empty-handed, no one need know the mission Ki had been on, or the role that Stalking Bear had played in it.

In settlements and frontier towns throughout the Southwest, it was common knowledge that a white man couldn't figure a Comanche. Whatever you reckoned the Indian would do, he would inevitably do the opposite. If you picked north, he went south. If you elected to stop, the Indian continued. Ki had heard all the stories but never agreed with the popular theory that held, "Injuns're jus' damned contrary or simply plain loco." Ki had always felt that they were actually being rather crafty. The Indian's way of fighting, even their way of survival, depended upon never being outguessed. They always had to keep their enemy, be it buffalo or army battalions, uncertain. Ki had always felt that it was only necessary to step into the Indians' moccasins to understand their strategy, but now as he sat across from Stalking Bear, he wondered if there might not be some truth to the popular school of thought.

Stalking Bear started to build a fire. It was not a meager fire meant only to heat a can of beans or a pot of coffee, but a healthy blaze intended to fight back the cold night winds. Of course there was no need for secrecy, Ki thought dryly. For once Ki could sleep on the plains and not worry about attacking Indians. But Ki noticed the Indian did not

101

spread out his blanket, and Ki assumed his rest would not include any sleep.

The Indian dug his hand into a pouch and passed a handful of thick paste to Ki. "Pemmican, good." He took a handful for himself, put it into his mouth, then closed the pouch.

Ki tasted the mixture of dried meats, animal fat, berries, and nuts and agreed it was good.

"In times of no buffalo, when the snows fall, we eat this for many moons," Stalking Bear explained.

Ki nodded. There were too many instances of trappers eating a steady diet of squirrel, dying of malnutrition during the winter months. To stave off the cold a body needed fat to burn, and the small rodents provided almost no fat for fuel. Ki licked his greasy fingers. There would be no chance a Comanche eating pemmican would ever die from lack of necessary animal fat.

Ki rewrapped his blanket around himself, tucked his feet on his lap, then began to stare into the fire. He watched the burning embers glow bright. They shimmered like precious jewels reflecting the sunlight. Ki intensified his stare, concentrating deeper into every facet of the jewel, transfixed by every burning flicker. His focus narrowed or the ember expanded, Ki didn't know which, but soon he was totally encompassed by the hot coal. He felt the warmth on his face trickle down and radiate out to the farthest corners of his being. He was awash in the heat and glow. His eyes focused on the infinite, his breathing slowed, his body rested.

Some time later, Ki refocused his attention. Stalking Bear was standing up and kicking dirt on the fire. Time to go. Ki rose feeling refreshed. His short meditation, judging from the position of the moon not much more than an hour, had been more beneficial than twice that amount of sleep. He swung back into the saddle and was once again following, and staring at, the large muscular back of Stalking Bear.

The dawn had broken and the sun was rising behind them. It offered light; the sky had slowly gone from a light shade of gray to bright orange, but it was still too low to offer any considerable warmth. It would be hours before Ki would feel the strong rays of the sun warming his back.

There was now enough light to start looking for signs, and Stalking Bear began to search the ground as they rode. He nodded to himself, then called to Ki. "Here. Little Knife was here." He pointed to a mound of small stones. "He was heading for the river. That way." The Comanche pointed. "Not far, but I don't think he made it."

"You can tell all that?" Ki said with surprise. He was a good sign reader, but the pile of stones meant nothing to him.

Stalking Bear smiled. "I do not read the track. I read the sign," he said enigmatically. Ki shook his head, not understanding. The Indian tried to explain again. He pointed to the pile of small rocks. "Little Knife tells me this. I read it . . . like a white man reads a marker."

Now Ki understood. The stones were a message, albeit a coded one. It would be important for members of any nomadic tribe to be able to leave messages warning of danger, or telling of herd or tribe movement. No wonder the Comanche had ridden the plains in undisputed rule for so many years. He was as at home out here as any white man was in a well-built town.

"He searches for buffalo along the river," Stalking Bear added.

"How do you know he never made it?" Ki asked.

"I was along the river, waiting. Then I go back."

"He was killed between here and the river?" It was not really a question.

The large Comanche nodded. "There is a house over there. A white man."

Stalking Bear apparently had no doubts, and Ki would not have been surprised if the house belonged to Partridge.

103

He was curious to see what kind of spread the man had. Would it be well-worked like the Caldwells' or would it be a front for a plug-ugly gunman?

Stalking Bear turned his horse and proceeded north. A few minutes later he stopped and pointed to the ground. "Blood. Not old."

Ki was amazed at the Indian's eyesight. He swung down from his horse to study the tuft of buffalo grass. He bent over . . . then everything went black.

Ki opened his eyes slowly and painfully. There was a powerful throbbing emanating from the back of his head. He reached up to feel the source of pain and realized his hands were tied behind his back. He looked for Stalking Bear, expecting to see the Indian tied next to him. Whoever jumped them must have also—

He stopped suddenly. The fog in his head cleared. There was no one who could have jumped them. No one could have sneaked up on them. There was only the Comanche. When Ki lowered his head to inspect the ground, Stalking Bear must have hit him with a heavy object. Ki focused his attention on the back of his neck, feeling mentally for a bleeding wound. He could detect no sticky warmth or matted hair to indicate his skin had been broken.

No, the Indian had hit him with an object sufficiently weighty to knock him out, yet padded enough not to break his skin. It was no mystery what the Indian had used. His powerful, meaty hands were perfect for the job. Sitting astride the horse, Stalking Bear only had to bring his hands together, raise them above his head, then bring them down quickly on the soft spot at the base of Ki's skull. Judging from the strength of the Comanche, Ki suspected he was out before he even hit the ground.

Before he pondered the next question—why Stalking Bear had attacked him—Ki took stock of the situation. He was lying on the floor of a one-room shack. Against the far wall there was a fireplace; opposite that was a wooden table and bench. A cot rounded out the room's furnishings. Obviously this was a white man's habitation. No Indian would use a table, bench, or cot. Why had Stalking Bear brought him here? There were many questions to be answered, but first Ki had to deal with his bonds.

The knot was well-tied, and his hands were held tightly together. If he had been conscious when his hands were tied, he might have been able to position his wrists in such a way that he would now have some slack in which to manuever. But Stalking Bear had placed his wrists flat together. Ki not only had no slack but was suffering from a lack of of circulation. The tips of his fingers were slightly numb. There was surely a way to free himself, but Ki had not yet hit upon it when the door opened and Stalking Bear stepped into the cabin.

"You are awake," the Indian remarked.

"How long have I been out?"

"That is of no matter. You are lucky you are alive," he said unemotionally. His huge hands dropped a bunch of twigs in the fireplace.

"You would rather have killed me?" Ki asked, fishing for information.

"I do not care. But alive you are a burden," Stalking Bear said as he lighted a match. The twigs caught fire quickly.

"And dead I am no problem," Ki finished the sentence for him. "So why do I still breathe, Stalking Bear?"

"I have no love for the white man, Spirit HalfBreed."

"I am not a white man," Ki objected. It was ironic that he would be considered a white man. Most white men viewed him as an Oriental heathen, and yet his Japanese family rejected him as being the product of a Western barbarian. It always struck Ki how difficult it was to walk the fence between the two worlds. Someone was always trying to push him off into the other side.

"You are not Comanche," Stalking Bear replied simply.

Ki was getting nowhere. He took another look around

the room and decided to take a chance. "If you have no love for the white man," he taunted, "why do you do his bidding?"

The Indian at first looked surprised, then drew his knife. For a moment Ki thought he had pushed the Comanche too far. But then Stalking Bear reached down behind the fireplace and picked up a tin can. He stabbed the knife into the top of the can. "I do the bidding of Stalking Bear and only Stalking Bear."

"Then why am I alive?" Ki asked again.

"To bait the woman," he said uncaringly, as he sat down before the fireplace.

Ki did not like the answer. Not only because he feared for Jessie's safety, but because it also boded poorly for his own. Stalking Bear would only tell him this if he knew that Ki's fate was sealed. For now there was a reason to keep Ki alive, but soon that reason would no longer exist, and then . . . Ki continued to struggle silently with his bonds, but he was getting nowhere. He had to keep Stalking Bear talking, for more information and more time. "Who gives you orders, Stalking Bear?"

The Indian lifted his eyes from the tin can. "The chicken does not ask the coyote questions," he said, then continued to work his knife around the edge of the can.

For a moment Ki considered trying to pull off another "mighty spirit" act, but he dismissed the idea. His mighty spirit had not kept him from being knocked cold by the Indian, and neither did it free him from his bonds. He didn't think the ruse would get far with the hulking warrior, who had just pried back the lid of the can and was now shoveling cold beans into his mouth with the blade of his knife. Ki struck out on another tack. "This white man will only bring your people to ruin."

Stalking Bear seemed uninterested. "There is no hope for my people. They could have listened to me once, but they turned away." He filled his mouth with more beans.

"Stalking Bear, what I said in the council I still believe. The woman and I can help your people."

The Comanche's anger flared. "You can not help! I can not help. No one can help." He pointed the knife at his chest. "I help myself. I take care of Stalking Bear."

With that one simple gesture, Ki suddenly understood. "I take care of myself." How often had Ki heard those very same words? Every pawn conned into doing someone else's dirty work used the same sentiment to justify their actions. But many a greedy, corrupt plug-ugly crook also mouthed the same words. Ki's eyes narrowed. For a brief moment he had thought Stalking Bear was only a dumb pawn being used for ends he did not fully understand, but now he saw things for the way they were. He was shocked at first to realize that Stalking Bear was selling out his people for his own benefit. He naturally assumed a strong solidarity existed among the Indians. But there were corrupt individuals in every society. Why shouldn't the Comanches have their bad apples as well? With Stalking Bear exposed, Ki could no longer control his feelings. "You killed Little Knife," Ki accused openly.

The Indian nodded. "He would have betrayed me. He was my friend, but there was no other way." Having finished the beans, Stalking Bear wiped his knife clean on his leather leggings and placed it back in its sheath.

Ki felt a strong revulsion toward this man who would betray his people and murder his friends. Though he was still tied and helpless, he couldn't let the Indian escape. When Stalking Bear rose to his feet, he knew he didn't have much time left. "One day the white man will kill you, like you killed Little Knife."

The Comanche turned to Ki and smiled slowly. "Stalking Bear is not that easy to kill." He stamped the small fire out quickly, then started to the door.

"You can't leave me here," cried Ki. "I'll freeze to death."

107

"You will not be here long. They will soon send someone for you."

"But without a fire, the cold . . ."

"You will have no fire to burn the ropes with, Spirit HalfBreed."

The Indian had seen through his plan immediately, but Ki did not show his disappointment. "Please, Stalking Bear, at least my blanket." Stalking Bear looked at him suspiciously. "What harm could a blanket do?" Ki pleaded.

Stalking Bear ignored him and walked out the door. Ki did not know if he was going for the blanket or not. He really didn't care. What he did care about was the tin can the Indian had carelessly left behind. Ki struggled to his feet. There was a sharp pain running from the base of his skull across his head, but after the initial stab the pain was endurable. Ki was grateful that Stalking Bear had not found it necessary to tie his feet. He walked over to the fireplace and used his foot to place the empty can next to the stone hearth. Sitting down with his back against the wall, his fingers took hold of the can. He maneuvered the can till he got the base wedged in against a rock and the serrated lid pointing up at his wrist.

Slowly he pressed his ropes against the sharpest edge and began to wriggle his wrists. The top of the can was sharp enough to cut through a single strand of cord. Ki had to make sure it would cut through the hundred or more strands that composed the rope. Periodically his hands would slip and one of the metal barbs would cut his palm. The first time it happened, he cursed softly. Not because of the pain, but for the unnecessary delay. It took time to reposition the can correctly, and Ki did not have time to waste. Every extra minute gave Stalking Bear a larger head start. He worked at the rope a little faster. Once he cut through enough strands he hoped he could snap the rope with sheer muscle and determination. He was just a strand of two short of that when he heard a horse ride up. Ki continued to work on his bonds, but very slowly and carefully, taking care not to let the can drop. He was hoping he could cut a little deeper even with someone in the room.

The door swung in and Stalking Bear entered. "Do not worry about freezing. You are coming with me. It will save me trouble later."

Apparently the Comanche thought Ki had moved over to the fireplace for a bit of warmth. But the minute he lifted Ki up he would know the truth. It was likely that Stalking Bear would then knock Ki out with another powerful blow of his fist. Ki had to strike while the element of surprise was his.

Stalking Bear stood over Ki and reached down to pull him to his feet. It was then that Ki struck. He threw himself backward; his leg shot up straight in the air. His foot caught the Comanche right in the balls. Two things happened. The Indian let out a curdling yell as he doubled over in pain, and Ki snapped his bonds. When he leaned back to lift his leg all his weight was pressed against the tin can. That little extra was all that was needed. His rope broke, and the can went rolling off into the center of the room.

Ki struck again quickly, but this time his *mae-geri-keage* had less of an effect. The powerful snap kick connected solidly with Stalking Bear's rib cage but didn't seem to penetrate the solid mass of the Indian. Fortunately Stalking Bear was still suffering the effects of Ki's first well-placed kick, and Ki had time for another strike.

The Indian's sheer bulk presented Ki with a formidable problem in itself—one that was further complicated by the fact that Ki wanted the Comanche alive. He had to find out who was giving Stalking Bear his orders. The Indian's time would no doubt come, but for now Ki had to be certain he extracted the necessary information. Although Indians were rarely treated as equals, death had a way of evening the score. Death silenced both red and white men alike. Dead men—including dead Indians—told no tales.

Ki would have liked another shot at the Comanche's

genitals, but Stalking Bear was hunched over in pain, effectively protecting his vulnerable spot from further assault. Ki lashed out with a roundhouse kick to the head. This time there was a reaction, though not an altogether positive one. The kick did not seem to do much damage, but it did shake Stalking Bear out of his painful fog. He glared at Ki, then rushed headlong at him.

There was little Ki could do. There was no time to out-maneuver or sidestep. Though Stalking Bear was huge, he was not slow and lumbering. He was on Ki almost immediately. Ki reached for the Indian's arm and tried to use Stalking Bear's lunging momentum to throw him to the ground, but with all his mass he was not easily pushed about.

Ki soon found himself locked in a deadly bear hug. Stalking Bear's strength allowed him to skip lightly over the finer points of combat. While his fellow braves were perfecting timing, movements, and form, Stalking Bear had relied on only two things: size and strength. Ki found it disconcerting to realize that all the speed and coordination in the world would not help once you were in this Comanche's deadly grasp. Stalking Bear had probably not lost many fights. The Indian's massive arms locked around Ki's body and threatened to squeeze the very life out of him. He could feel the enormous pressure against his rib cage. Only proper breathing and deep lung expansion kept Ki's rib cage from cracking like a pile of so many brittle twigs. But he did not know how long he could stave off the inevitable.

He jabbed repeatedly at Stalking Bear's midriff, but his elbow strokes had no effect. Ki could feel his strength slowly fading away. He would only have enough for one or two more maximum-effort strikes. Stalking Bear could feel Ki weakening. He seemed to squeeze even harder, though Ki wondered if that was actually possible. As Stalking Bear increased his effort, he arched his back and lifted Ki

110

another few inches off the ground. Instantly Ki hoped he had a target. It was his last resort. It had to work.

Ki pointed his fingers and brought them tightly together. Each hand looked vaguely like the beak of a bird. He focused his attention on the points of each hand, his fingers now hard as iron spikes. He was ready for his last effort, a *yonhon-nukite,* or spear-hand strike. He quickly thrust his hands up and behind him, aiming for the Comanche's eyes. One hand crunched painfully against a solid surface, probably the Indian's forehead. Ki suspected he might have broken one of his fingers. But the other hand dug deep into something soft and moist. There was a loud howl. Ki knew he had found the Indian's eye socket.

The Comanche did not totally release his hold. He dropped one arm and brought it up to his face, but the other arm still held Ki. The balance, though, had shifted. Ki now had the advantage. He swung a leg behind the Indian and threw all his weight against the veritable mountain of Indian flesh. The Comanche teetered, then fell. As they hit the ground, Stalking Bear's arm went slack. Ki rolled away and sprung to his feet. The Indian lay on the floor, the tin can embedded deeply into his temple.

Stalking Bear was still breathing, but he was seriously wounded. Ki rushed outside to see if there were two horses. There were. He raced to get his blanket. Maybe if he could stop the bleeding and keep the Indian warm, he might live. Ki hurried back into the cabin, but as he stepped up to the door, Stalking Bear loomed in front of him. The Indian moved slowly, the tin can still protruding obliquely from the side of his head. The lid was in deeper than half its diameter and bright red blood was flowing freely down the Comanche's face. Stalking Bear's eyes were screwed up in pain, but he moved steadily toward Ki. It was a gruesome sight. Ki stepped back. He was wondering what to do next—any blow might be fatal—when the Indian stumbled and fell forward. Stalking Bear hit the ground with a solid thump. The can rattled and rolled

111

away, taking a sizable chunk from the side of the Indian's head. Ki bent over the Comanche. This time there was no life left in Stalking Bear.

Unlike the other day, as Ki rode through the Comanche village he created quite a stir. He headed directly for the tepee that had held the council. By the time he and his packhorse, laden down with the corpse of Stalking Bear, reached the tepee, there was a large crowd of braves. He looked for Black Elk but did not find him. He slid down from his mount, and another elderly Indian stood before him. The man shouted out commands in Comanche, and there was a stir among the braves. Ki recognized the man from the council. Like Black Elk, his face was also heavily lined and his hair hung low, but it was gray and lifeless. As he had in council, he wore many beads and a necklace of bear claws and eagle talons. Ki assumed he was the medicine man and now in charge. He turned to face him directly. "Stalking Bear has betrayed you."

The medicine man barked out another order. Ki could not understand the flurry of activity around him, but could easily understand the buzz that would naturally accompany Stalking Bear's death. "He murdered Little Knife . . ."

The medicine man raised his hand. Suddenly, before Ki could utter another word, a lance was thrust in his face. From the corner of his eye, he could see another brave standing with weapon at the ready. Ki could also practically feel the spear point that he knew was just inches from the back of his head. And as if that weren't enough, there were a handful of Indian archers surrounding him from a distance, their arrows nocked, bowstrings pulled back.

Chapter 11

By midmorning Lieutenant Stafford and his two soldiers overtook the lone rider. "Morning, Miss Starbuck," the lieutenant said with a tip of his hat. There was a naughty twinkle in his eye. "Nice day for a ride, but you're a little far from the reservation."

It took all of Jessie's efforts to resist smiling. "I'm heading out to the Caldwells', Lieutenant," she said nonchalantly.

"There may be some Indian trouble afoot. It'd be best if we rode along with you."

"I'd be honored, sir." With that, Stafford brought his horse alongside Jessie's, and the two cavalrymen fell in behind.

Jessie and Stafford exchanged occasional pleasantries throughout the ride. There were other, more important, things Jessie wished to discuss with the handsome officer, but she felt self-conscious with the two other men riding along. Although few words passed between them, as the miles slipped by Jessie felt herself becoming more and more comfortable with Stafford. Every word or smile they shared seemed to have a special meaning.

They stopped at noon to feed the horses and themselves. One of the soldiers built a fire while the other pulled out a small pot and started some water to boil. As they sipped at their coffee a few minutes later, Stafford turned to Jessie. "If you wouldn't mind, Jessie, I was thinking of maybe swinging up north."

"But the Caldwells' house is that way." She pointed southwest. "I did intend to warn them, Stafford."

"I know, but there are quite a few homesteaders around the Moss River. I thought we'd swing around and hit the Caldwells' on our way back."

Jessie smiled. "I know your tricks, Lieutenant Stafford. You just want me along for the company, and you're afraid if we hit the Caldwells' place first I'll turn around and head straight home." Stafford grinned broadly, and Jessie was pleased that she hadn't let the cocky officer pull anything over on her. "You simply should ask. Why, I'd be pleased to ride along. I'd like to see who these other homesteaders are."

Stafford was still smiling, but his eyes were serious. "Ma'am, there ain't no denying I'd like to have you ride along. And maybe I'd be a mite bit shy to ask outright, but that ain't the reason for heading north first."

Jessie could tell he was no longer playing a courting game. "If there's a good reason, I wouldn't—".

"There's a good reason, all right. The Comanches, at least the tribe we have at Three Rivers, used to roam up north. Before we put them on the reservation they wintered up in the Crystal Mountains."

Jessie nodded her head. "I see."

Stafford continued. "If there's any trouble, I reckon the Indians'll head back that way."

"You're right. We should warn those homesteaders first." She changed her tone. "You seem to know a bit about the Comanches," she wondered out loud.

"Why shouldn't I?" Stafford asked defensively.

"Well, you didn't seem too sympathetic," Jessie began.

"Just 'cause I don't like 'em don't mean I don't know a thing or two about 'em." Jessie couldn't tell if he was truly offended or just teasing her. "Hell, I know my business," he added emphatically.

Jessie realized he wasn't playing. "For someone who wouldn't ride up to the Indian camp with me, you sure are taking offense." As soon as she said it she was sorry. Jessie suspected that it might be a low blow, but when she saw the hurt in the young man's eyes she knew she had gone too far.

The lieutenant rose to his feet crisply, all business. "Let's mount up," he ordered. "This ain't no pleasure outing." He was saying it to no one in particular, but he was looking straight at Jessie.

The sun had started to set and the frost between the two had still not thawed. Stafford dismounted when they reached a small grove of walnut trees, and his men followed suit. "I hope you don't mind spending a night outside under the stars, Miss Starbuck? We're only a few hours from the first homestead, but I'd rather show up in the morning than go surprising them in the middle of the night."

"That's fine with me, Lieutenant." It came out more cut-and-dried than she had intended. "Makes good sense, Stafford," she added warmly, but it had little effect.

Dinner was a typical trail meal of jerked beef, beans, and biscuits. The coffee was bitter but hot. Jessie did not mind the sparse victuals as much as she minded the cold atmosphere. Stafford had turned her off and shut her out. Though she didn't totally understand it, she couldn't say she blamed him. For an officer to be embarrassed in front of his men was bad enough. To have the insult come at the hands of a woman was worse. And if the woman was young and sexy, as she was in this case, it was that much worse. Jessie wanted to apologize, but she also wanted to know why Stafford was so damned touchy on the subject of Indians. She hoped she would get a chance to talk to him in private. But for now she settled back to watch the last colors of sunset bleed away at the horizon.

In the summer, there were often spectacular sunsets, and even clear winter days could have brilliant displays, though often they were dull and lackluster, the light gradually fading till the shades of gray were eventually replaced by dark black. Periodically, however, somewhere between the dull and the dark, the horizon would light up in warm tones of red and orange. Tonight's sunset was one of these. Along the horizon, the light of the already vanished sun was reflected in a thin band of glowing color. Overhead the sky was dark enough for the first stars to begin twinkling, but at the horizon there was the brilliant stab of red that stretched up and out to the coming night. It looked as if a streak of blood were flung across the horizon. Jessie smiled. Many a small child believed the sun crashed into the ground and filled the sky with its blood. They went to sleep hoping the sun was not hurt, that it would be well again by morning. Jessie had been no exception. She had always woken up and looked to the sky, thankful for the sun's speedy recovery. She smiled again at the thought, and noticed that Stafford too was watching the sunset. She thought she saw a trace of a smile around the corners of his mouth.

The color didn't last long, and when it faded, night was quickly upon them. It always amazed Jessie how dark night could be on the prairie. The moon was either not up yet or behind low clouds, for there was no light in the sky. Of course, on a clear night with a full moon, it could often be bright enough to read a book, or at least see which end of the book was up.

"You both can bed down," Stafford addressed his men. "I'll take the first watch, ma'am." He got up and took his Winchester with him. Jessie heard him lever a cartridge as he walked over to check on the horses. She lay down on her bedroll, though she knew sleep wouldn't come easily. She didn't know how long she'd been staring up at the sky

116

when she was roused by the sound of a soldier snoring. It was possible only a few minutes had passed. After a whole day's ride beginning at dawn, a man with a clear conscience could be fast asleep in minutes. Jessie got up quietly. She half-wondered if she had been waiting for the two soldiers to fall asleep. After all, she hadn't slipped into her bedroll. But this seemed like a good time to seek out Stafford and set things right.

She walked quietly, but not too much so. When she heard something stir she called out softly, "It's me—Jessie."

"Over here," came the quiet reply. Jessie followed the voice to the last of the trees. From here one could see out onto the prairie for quite a ways. Even on a dark night, the spot offered an unobstructed vantage point from which to hear the sounds of the night—whether natural, man-made, or Indian-made. She saw the lieutenant sitting with his back against the tree, his blanket wrapped around his shoulders.

"Stafford, about this afternoon, I want to say I'm truly sorry," she whispered as she stood above him.

"No need, Jessie. I think I owe you an apology, or at least an explanation. Sit down." Jessie sat, and Stafford continued to talk, though he looked off into the distance and not at her. "We don't see eye to eye about Indians."

"We don't have to agree on everything, Stafford," she said, though she did wish the officer showed more compassion for the Indians.

"That doesn't bother me much," he continued. "But I reckoned maybe I should reconsider the whole affair."

"How so?"

"I always see things one way, my way. But there are two sides to a silver dollar."

"My father always said to understand somebody, even your enemy, you had to put yourself in his shoes."

"Or moccasins," he added with forced good humor. But his voice grew softer and raspier, as if the words were

117

hardly formed in his throat. "But I don't have a father. Least not one I knew." Jessie placed her hand on his thigh. "I was a baby when my family was settling on the Kansas River. They were all killed in an Indian raid. I was taken captive."

Jessie found her words were also thick in her throat. "You don't have to go on."

Stafford placed his hand over Jessie's. "There's not much to tell. I really don't remember anything." Despite his calm tones Jessie could feel a slight tremor in his hand. "My uncle, my father's brother, ransomed me a few days later, then moved his whole family, an' me, back to St. Louis."

"I didn't know," Jessie said softly.

"How could you? Anyways, no one knows." He shrugged. "Most of the time, I don't even think about it myself. I was too young to remember my real family, and my uncle gave me a good home." He hesitated briefly. "It's just sometimes I get these feelings when I'm around the Comanches, or up at their village. Deep inside me I think there are these memories that are locked up trying to come out. Sometimes I can almost feel myself sinking into the quicksand."

"I know what you mean, Stafford. When we were holed up at the Caldwells' fighting what I thought were Indians, I felt the same way. Hot, and dizzy, and confused. I think I was remembering a night when the ranch was attacked by Indians."

"What happened?" Stafford asked as he now squeezed her hand. There was deep concern in his voice.

Jessie smiled. "I don't know. I was very little. I don't remember anything either."

"Are you making fun of me, Miss Starbuck?"

"Oh, no . . ." Jessie said earnestly. She hoped she had not hurt his feelings, then stopped and broke out into a soft laugh when she realized this time Stafford was teasing her.

118

"It's funny how those things we can't remember haunt us so."

"I think that's the way it works. We're afraid of things we don't know. Things different and strange and foreign."

Stafford let go of her hand and brought it up against her cheek. He could feel her soft hair falling against the back of his hand. For an instant he had an uncontrollable urge to bury his face into her soft mane. "You're different than any woman I've ever known, Jessie."

Jessie wanted to ask how many woman he had known, but resisted the urge. That didn't matter to her, though she was sure a good-looking cavalry officer had known his share of good times. Instead she simply said, "Thank you."

Stafford continued to stroke her hair. "You're different, but I don't seem afraid of you. I don't have bad dreams about you."

"What kind of dreams do you have about me?"

"What makes you think I dream about you at all?" he said with a grin.

"Well, do you?" Jessie asked coyly.

"Sometimes I dream about kissing you."

"And . . . ?" Jessie prompted. "Is that all you do— dream?"

Stafford leaned forward and pressed his lips against hers. Gently at first, then more insistently as Jessie slowly parted her lips. They kissed deeply, Stafford's tongue dancing over Jessie's. Slowly she pulled away and caught her breath. "Is that how it is in your dreams?"

"I can't say I'm disappointed."

"But is that all you dream about?" Jessie asked as she wrapped her arms around his neck and moved closer to him. Even through her heavy coat she could feel her breasts pressing up against him.

"Sometimes I dream about your head on my shoulder, your hair against my chest." He swallowed and continued. "And your breasts soft in my hands." He inched away from her, but just enough to unbutton her coat and slip his hands

119

against her bosom. Through her cotton blouse he could feel her nipples harden. He grabbed the bud between his thumb and finger and pressed gently.

Jessie moaned softly. "I think I like your dreams." She leaned forward and met his lips with hers, then let her tongue explore his mouth. His hands kept kneading the firm soft flesh of her breasts, till he replaced his hands with his mouth, and let his tongue flick quickly over her erect nipple.

"But in my dreams, we're inside, and there's a nice warm fire."

"I don't feel the least bit cold, Stafford."

"You would if I undressed you and laid you out under the moonlight."

She reached for the bulge in his pants. "If that's all you did I might feel cold, but . . ." Through the cloth she felt him harden. Stafford let out a soft groan. It could have been one of pleasure or one of pain. The confinement of his pants might be causing his manhood extreme discomfort. Jessie began undoing his trouser buttons. She wouldn't want his manly tool to be cramped inside his pants. But she also wanted to feel his flesh in her hands, then deep inside her. She wasn't just being accommodating when she said the cold didn't bother her. In fact she was feeling quite warm. Starting from deep inside of her the warmth spread out and encompassed her.

Stafford must have been feeling the same heat. He cradled her in his arms and pressed her flat against the cold ground. He worked feverishly at her pants till he had them undone and around her knees. It was then that the moon emerged from behind the clouds. Stafford sighed in delight. Her creamy thighs shone desert-white in the pale light, and her soft mound glistened with beads of her deep desire. "You are beautiful, Jessie. I could look at you forever," he promised, but he lowered his head and kissed her soft, well-shaped thighs.

"I need you to keep me warm," she purred as she

reached behind his head and pulled his mouth up to hers. They kissed again hungrily, and Jessie reached out and grabbed his rigid rod, guiding it to the soft mound between her legs. Stafford pressed his body weight against her, but Jessie held fast, not permitting him to enter her yet. She continued to stroke him, but at the same time worked the soft tip of his shaft against her tiny pleasure button.

Stafford didn't seem to mind the delay. He kissed her neck gently and pushed back her blouse, slowly lowering his head to her soft mounds. He opened his mouth wide and sucked on her full breast. Jessie sighed, her fingers slipping away from his manhood. Then she let out a gasp. With one powerful thrust Stafford entered her, penetrating to the hilt. Jessie spread her knees to accommodate his huge organ, but her legs were hampered by the pants that hung around her knees. She would have liked to have asked him to remove her pants totally, but she couldn't form the words in her throat. Stafford's hips thrust relentlessly, and her body responded in kind. Her pelvis rocked back and forth to his every motion. Her breath came in deep gulps; even if she had found conversation possible she didn't think she would want Stafford to stop even for a moment. Even with her leg movement confined she could feel herself rushing helplessly toward orgasmic bliss. She considered trying to check the flow; to ask Stafford to rest a moment and give her a chance to catch her breath, but she could feel the cold of the night touching her in the places that Stafford's body did not. Goose bumps were coming out on her back, her bottom, and her knees. Besides, if Stafford kept up his rhythmic movements there would be no chance to stem the tide, and Jessie had no desire to.

Her muscles began to clasp his manhood, gripping tight, increasing the friction. Stafford moaned once, then continued to moan with every thrust. "I can't hold back, Stafford, I can't control it."

He responded with an even greater passion. Jessie could

take no more. The feeling stampeded forth, her musc[l]
contracted mightily. Her body shook. Stafford plunge[d]
deep, then exploded himself. Jessie wondered if her eye[s]
really bulged or if they just felt like they did. She smile[d]
and concentrated on the spasms that racked her body. For [a]
moment she couldn't differentiate between his twitchin[g]
manhood and her squeezing sheath. They shook and vi[-]
brated together.

Stafford was still hard as he pulled out. "I don't wan[t]
you to freeze," he said as he pulled up her pants.

Jessie did not argue. "I think I'd like that warm fire
now. I'd like to hold you next to me and make you fee[l]
good again and again and again."

"You've already made me feel terrific, Jessie. I can'[t]
imagine what else you could possibly do."

She took hold of his shaft. It was still massive, but was
quickly shrinking due to the cold. She leaned forward and
blew her soft breath against its tender skin. "It's not only
what else I can do, Stafford"—her tongue snaked out
across his dripping tip— "but how long I can do it for."

"I'm sorry we were so rushed, Jessie."

Jessie smiled. "I can't say I'm disappointed," she said,
mocking his earlier comment.

"Even if we weren't out in the cold in the middle of
nowhere, with me standing watch, I don't think I could
have controlled myself any better."

"I'll take that as a compliment, Lieutenant."

"I've been dreaming about this too much."

"Why, Mason Stafford!" she exclaimed. "And I thought
you only dreamed about a kiss and a hug."

He smiled unembarrassedly. "But next time I'm going to
hold you to your word, and we'll take our time."

"And a warm fire?"

"It's a promise," the officer assured her.

"Good. Then *I'll* have something to dream about."

But for some reason Jessie did not dream about Stafford; she dreamed about Ki, and it was not a happy dream.

Though she woke up not remembering the details, a strong premonition stayed with her. As she sipped her morning coffee, she waited for the feelings to fade. But they did not. By the time the horses were saddled she made up her mind. "Stafford, I'm going back."

He looked shocked. "But why?" There was a deep disappointment in his voice. He walked around to the other side of his horse. Their conversation could now be conducted with some semblance of privacy.

Jessie could almost read his mind. "It has nothing to do with last night," she said softly. "It's Ki."

The look of surprise remained on Stafford's face. "But I thought you said he was only a friend."

She nodded. "But I think he's a friend in need."

"What's wrong? What's happened?"

"I don't know. I just have this awful feeling. I want to get back as fast as I can."

"Jessie, this doesn't make sense."

"I don't care if it makes sense or not, Stafford." She swung up into her saddle.

"Ki can take care of himself. I'm sure he's all right," he said as he put a comforting hand on her leg.

"You're probably right," she said, though she didn't really believe it. "But I won't relax until I know that for sure."

Stafford could see there was no changing her mind. He climbed atop his horse and turned to her. "Then I'm going back with you."

"There's no need to, Stafford."

"I know that."

"But what about your duties?"

"O'Rourke and Hensen can carry them out fine without me."

"But there'll be hell to pay when you get back," she reasoned. "I'll be fine by myself."

Stafford smiled and shook his head. "I think I can deal with McKenzie and whatever he chooses to dish out as punishment better than I could with something happening to you."

"Do you think something might happen?" She wondered about that herself. If Ki had been successful in his dealings with the Indians there would probably be no trouble. But If everything had gone smoothly, why did she have this bad premonition about Ki's welfare and safety?

"I don't know, Jessie," he said with a shrug. "But it's not worth taking a chance. I'd be punishing myself for the rest of my life if I didn't go with you and something happened."

Jessie saw his mind was made up. In a way she was glad. Not so much for the protection he offered during the ride back, but for what might be in store farther down the way. If Ki were in trouble she would be glad to have the lieutenant's help. She nodded to him. "I understand, Stafford," she said simply.

The lieutenant turned to his men and gave them instructions. For a brief moment he was concerned with their safety, but then, Jessie alone would be in more danger than these two soldiers would be. He cautioned his men to be on the alert, then didn't give it another thought. He slipped his Winchester from its boot and eased it back in, making sure it would slip out quickly if needed. He settled himself into his saddle and turned to see if Jessie was ready. She nodded. "Let's ride!" he ordered, then spurred his horse into a gallop.

★

Chapter 12

Ki soon found himself in the lodge tepee, lying facedown on a buffalo skin. It was not the most restful of positions; his hands were once again securely tied behind his back. This time, though, with some simple manipulation and some not-so-simple distortion of the muscles in his hands he would, with time, be free. But that was not the problem. His goal was to get the Comanches to trust and believe him. If he were to escape he would lose whatever credibility he might have earned. Still, he did not relish the idea of remaining tied for any length of time. Besides, he could think better with his hands free.

Eventually he wriggled free of his bonds. Having nothing else to do, he studied the tepee. After spending some time in the Indian lodging he was amazed how comfortable it was. The fire in the center of the tepee was snuffed out when he was thrown in the tent, yet he was still warm. The sides of the tent were draft free, and unlike most tents he had been in, there was no precipitation forming on the inside of the walls. He guessed this was due to a second hide that covered the bottom half of the tepee walls and formed an inner skin. He marveled at the simple but effective design that allowed the tent to "breathe" and let air circulate freely. Smoke would never fill the tepee, and even in the summer months, Ki suspected, with the bottom of the flaps rolled up to allow even more air to circulate, the inside would stay moderately cool.

The thick buffalo hide he was lying on was soft and warm and as comfortable as most beds, and probably more so than many of the lumpy mattresses he had slept on in flea-ridden second-class hotels. The buffalo skins were also relatively easy to keep free of vermin. Ki was suddenly more determined than ever to fight for the Indian cause. But just now he didn't know how best to accomplish that. Having no better plan of action he closed his eyes and drifted off to sleep.

He awoke at the sound of the tepee flap being pushed back. He quickly placed his hands behind his back. It was now dark in the tent and the intruder could not have seen his quick movement, though the sound of his rustling would have been heard clearly. He lay there and waited.

"You are awake?" came a soft feminine voice. Ki remained silent till he knew who his visitor was. "I think I am your friend, Spirit HalfBreed. Do not make noise."

The voice came closer, and Ki could see a young Comanche woman. His eyes pierced the darkness slowly. He could make out the round face, and the long, straight hair. He couldn't see much else, but he sensed she was young and pretty.

"Why did you return here after killing Stalking Bear?"

"I did not kill him," Ki stated flatly.

"Then why did you come back?" the Indian asked again, as she knelt beside him.

Ki proceeded to tell her all about Stalking Bear's betrayal and the situation he believed the Comanches were being manipulated into. All the while the woman remained silent and listened.

When he finished the squaw nodded her head slowly. "Your arms must be tired. If I loosen the ropes you will not escape?"

"You do not have to worry about that," Ki said softly. He did not get a chance to explain before she had moved

126

over him and rolled him onto his side. As she moved to undo the knots, Ki could feel her breasts pressing against his shoulders. She smelled faintly musklike, an aroma probably caused by her suede leather clothing. It was not unpleasant. Ki felt a stirring in his loins.

Of course she realized immediately that he had slipped out of his ropes. "Are your legs also free?" she asked as she slipped her hands down to his ankles. "Why do you not try to escape?" she asked once she felt no ropes tying his legs.

"I do not want to escape, I want to help the *numinu.*"

Even in the dark he could see her smile. The squaw slowly ran her fingers up Ki's leg. It was not without its effect, which the Indian woman soon realized as her hand brushed across his crotch. She could not have helped but feel the large bulge in Ki's pants, but she did not seem surprised. Her fingers played lightly with his sack, and even through the pants Ki found it quite enjoyable. "You are a friend to the *numinu*, I will see how good a friend." Deftly she slipped Ki's pants off him, and his engorged member sprung free. Using both hands she began stroking his lengthy rod.

"What is your name?" Ki asked in a husky voice.

"Does it matter?" she responded coyly, never ceasing the rhythmic movements on Ki's shaft.

"No, not really, but . . ."

"It is best you do not know who I am." She let go of Ki to pull her shirt over her head. She then slipped Ki's shirt up and lowered her torso onto his flat, muscular stomach. Her mouth was only inches from the tip of his shaft, and Ki could feel her warm breath against him.

"I should know who you are, so one day I can repay your kindness."

"You can repay it here, now, Spirit Half Breed," she said as she swung her legs over his head, and hiked up her leather skirt.

Ki realized that her musky aroma was not solely due to

127

her clothes. Her deep feminine smell hovered over his head. Her body began to gyrate slowly, and the long silky hair that lay between her legs brushed lightly over his face. As she moved he was also aware that the hard nipples of her small, childlike breasts were tickling his stomach, but he was most keenly aware of her mouth. Her warm breath was replaced by her wet mouth, and Ki found his manhood deep inside her throat. For a moment or two he was lost in the pleasurable sensation, but was soon drawn out of it by the warm, sticky moisture that was coating his face.

He wrapped his arms around the squaw's waist, pulling up her skirt as he dug his fingers into her muscular buttocks. She responded by thrusting harder against his face. Ki stuck out his tongue into the dark folds of her wet crack. She moaned, and the vibration in her throat sent a tremor through Ki's shaft. Ki licked again, and the Comanche moaned once more. Ki pressed his tongue deeply into the woman, then flicked it lightly across her swollen pleasure point. Every move of his tongue sent a ripple through the woman's body. The pleasure she felt between her legs was echoed directly by the motion of her head and hands. As Ki caused her delight, her tongue brought equal ecstasy to his now throbbing pole. Soon it was indistinguishable who initiated and who reacted. Their two bodies rippled as one.

Ki thought the Indian would surely choke on his length. He seemed to be swelling to unusual proportions under her expert ministrations, yet at the same time he buried himself deeper into her soft mound of flesh. Her body shook with increased excitement, and the tension inside his loins rose to the bursting point. Ki did not realize who broke through first, who triggered whom. Suddenly the squaw's legs clamped tightly around his head, her knees pressing hard together. At the same instant Ki erupted deep inside her throat. His spasms subsided as the woman's tremors slowly eased.

They lay like that a minute before the Comanche woman pivoted around to lie face-to-face on top of Ki.

128

"Dark Cloud and the others speak of your powers," she said with a soft laugh, "but they do not know."

"You are of an equal power," Ki said as he ran his nails up her smooth back and through her hair.

"I do not think so, Spirit HalfBreed." Her hand reached behind her and found his still-tumescent organ. With one smooth motion she slid herself down onto it.

Ki sought and found her mouth, kissing her passionately as she engulfed his rod. As their tongues entwined, the Indian ran her fingers through his hair. "Your hair is like ours," she said as they separated for air.

"We are not so different," Ki answered. "We share many things."

"We share the spirit between us," she said as her hips began a slow rotation around Ki's now rock-hard pole.

Ki did not answer. He had no desire to talk. Without slipping out, he swung on top of her, and drove into her with a mighty thrust. She gasped, but met his movement. With increased speed and force he continued to drive into her. Under him the squaw lifted her ankles high into the air. From the sound of her forced breath, he knew she would not be long in climaxing.

"I have seen mighty stallions ride like this," she said, but soon her words turned into low growls of pleasure. Ki was relentless; every thrust racked her body with another wave of pleasure. "Your lance!" she exclaimed. "Your lance will kill me, but I will die gladly. Do not stop," she pleaded.

"I will not stop till you have released," Ki assured her.

"I want to scream, I must scream . . ." she gasped loudly. Her hips began bucking wildly. Ki lowered himself onto her and drove even deeper into her. Her mouth clamped onto his neck, her teeth sinking into his flesh. Her body stiffened, then went limp.

Ki now focused all his attention on his own sensations. The woman's warmth engulfed him, her moisture greased his rod, her muscles held him tightly. He slid slowly into her, feeling every inch that surrounded him. He drove as deeply as he could; when his lance could go no further, he released.

He could see the Comanche woman smiling. "One day when I am old and gray, I will tell of this."

Ki smiled at her. He only hoped her people would survive long enough for her to have that opportunity. But he did not say so.

The squaw was gone long before dawn, making sure to retie his hands before going. Ki realized the sense in that; the next Comanche to find him untied might not be as understanding or as friendly as the woman had been. And now as Running Wolf barged into the tepee Ki was doubly glad his hands were tied. He did not think the warrior would understand that even though his hands were untied, he was not trying to escape.

"Your fate is still in the hands of the council," the Indian informed him. "I speak on your behalf, as does Dark Cloud. I do not think you would kill, then deny it. But that is not for me to judge."

"Thank you, Running Wolf. But I am not only concerned with my fate. I care about the fate of your people. I want to be sure you do not make a mistake."

"Those decisions are already made," Running Wolf said as he grabbed Ki by the elbow and pulled him to his feet. "We have had enough of the white man's ways. We are leaving now." The Comanche led Ki out of the tent.

It was still an hour before sunrise, but the Indian village, or more precisely what was left of it, was alive with activity. Most of the tepees had already been pulled down, the others were in the process of being dismantled.

"I will leave you with my family. You will not try to escape, Spirit HalfBreed?" Ki nodded his assurance. "Good," the Indian said as he let go of Ki's elbow. "Though I speak for you, I would not hesitate to run my lance through you."

Ki did not bother to explain that he had no interest in escaping. His only goal was to get the Comanches to listen to reason. But as he looked around him he saw the time for listening was at an end. In just the few moments that Ki stood outside he saw two squaws dismantle a tepee. It was a quick job to roll up the hides and pull the tent poles. While the hides were strapped to a horse, two of the poles were attached behind another horse to form a large travois for hauling other bundles. It was a necessity of nomadic life for hunters like the Comanches to be easily mobile, yet the smooth efficiency Ki saw around him impressed him nevertheless.

As each family finished loading they started out on the trail. Only a few minutes separated the first from the last. Among whites, there were those who lived in mansions while others lived in shacks, but among Indians class was not determined by the number of expensive possessions. Riches were numbered in horses and hides, and a gallant warrior would make a family wealthy. But Ki noted dryly that even here there were those like Stalking Bear who wanted more, and were not above lying or cheating their fellow man to satisfy their own greed.

Ki had no more time to dwell on this. Running Wolf's family was packed and ready to move, and Ki soon found himself in line following a travois that carried an old lady and two small infants. The procession moved silently north, and in the predawn gloom Ki had the distinctly uncomfortable feeling that he was joining a long funeral march.

At first Jessie thought she had the wrong spot. She even wanted to believe that somehow she had gotten lost. Anything was better than admitting the obvious truth. But there was no mistaking the signs around them: the fire pits, the tepee markings, the cut brush. Although the land was now empty, just a short while ago this was the site of the Comanche village.

"Where'd they go?" Stafford wondered aloud.

"I don't know," Jessie answered as she slid off her horse to inspect the remains of a fire. "But they must have left early this morning," she added as she let the cold embers drop through her fingers.

"I reckon this is the start of it all, once Colonel McKenzie gets wind of this. Too bad Ki didn't have any better luck with 'em."

With the mention of Ki's name, Jessie's anxiety returned. "I'm going to race over to the Beckers', but I don't think Ki will be there."

"Where would he be?"

Jessie shrugged. "Wherever they are," she said as she gestured to the vacant site.

"Of his own free will?" Stafford sounded surprised.

"I don't know."

At the Becker house Jessie's suspicions were confirmed; Ki was nowhere in sight. When Lucy Becker asked if everything was all right, Jessie said things were fine. She made no mention of the Indians leaving the reservation.

Once outside Stafford questioned her on this. "Why are you keeping it a secret from them? They'll find out soon enough."

"I'd like to keep it a secret from everyone," she replied sternly.

"But, Jessie . . ." he started with a smile.

"I'm not kidding, Stafford. Once the cavalry goes after them we'll have a full-scale Indian war on our hands."

"I don't see how we can prevent that." There seemed to be a genuine tone of regret in his voice. "McKenzie's not going to sit still and let the Indians march out of here."

"Unless, of course, he doesn't know anything about it."

"Jessie, a whole Indian village just gets up and goes, an' you want to keep it a secret!"

"Only for a short time. Seems to me the army doesn't come up here all that much. It might be days before anyone realizes what's happened."

"By tomorrow, they'll know," Stafford said flatly.

Jessie studied the lieutenant. "You're not planning on telling, are you, Stafford?" Her voice was level, but her eyes looked worried.

Stafford took off his hat and pushed his hair back. "That's not what I meant, Jessie. I just think something will happen. Someone will get suspicious. There'll be no smoke, no Indians straying into the fort." Jessie still looked uncertain. Stafford smiled and took hold of her hand. "Besides, Lieutenant Stafford is out warning the homesteaders."

"And it wouldn't look good for an up-and-coming cavalry officer to desert his men," she added with a faint smile.

"You don't seem too relieved, Jessie."

"I'm not. I keep thinking of the army charging into the Indians. I don't think anyone will bother to notice whether they're shooting a full-blooded Comanche or a dark-haired half-Japanese."

There was no doubt as to her next course of action. Jessie had to follow the trail of the Indians and find Ki. Jessie turned to Stafford and announced boldly, "I'm going to stock up on provisions and head out after the Comanches."

"I'm going with you, Jessie."

Jessie started to shake her head but stopped. "I want you to, Stafford, but I want to be sure you know what you're getting into."

"I'm not a kid, Jessie. I've seen more'n my share of trouble, an' I can handle a fight."

There was no boast to his words. Jessie had never been fooled by his soft smile. A man doesn't become a lieutenant in the U.S. Cavalry unless he can take care of himself. But that was not what Jessie was thinking of. "If things go sour you may be caught between the two sides," she said flatly.

"I realize that," the lieutenant responded quickly.

"It could mean the end of your military career."

He hesitated briefly before answering. "It won't be the end of the world," he said as he gazed deep into Jessie's eyes.

Jessie swallowed. She didn't want to mislead the young officer. "About last night," she began tentatively. "I don't want you to think that there has to be any commitment."

"Last night, let me see . . ." The lieutenant scratched his head in thought. "I do seem to remember not getting much sleep. . . ."

"Stafford!" She tried to say it harshly, but the word was surrounded with a good-natured smile. "I just want to be sure you aren't doing this because of last night."

The lieutenant straightened and stood a good two inches taller. He addressed Jessie in a very businesslike manner. "Ma'am, I'm a professional soldier. I've had ladies hike up their petticoats for me in every frontier town this side of the Mississippi."

"I'm glad to hear it, Lieutenant," Jessie said crossly. "Thanks for putting me in my place," she added as she turned away.

"Aw, Jessie, I was only teasing," he said as he ran after her. He grabbed her by the arm. "Of course I'm doing it for you, but not because of anything that happened between us. I'm doing it not because I feel obligated to but because you're in a jam, and I think I can help."

Jessie looked into his eyes. She was surprised how much his cocky joke had hurt her but was now also moved by his sincerity. "Stafford, we could be risking our lives. I'm doing this for Ki. He's a very dear friend—"

The lieutenant did not let her finish. "Any friend of yours is a friend of mine," he said simply. Then he smiled to add a final punctuation to his words.

They walked back to the Beckers', where Lucy was glad to give them all the provisions they needed, no questions asked. Jessie had earned the Quaker woman's trust the ight Yellow Deer and her sick baby had come to the house. Lucy would not violate that trust now by prying into Jessie's affairs.

"Do you think we'll really need all this food we're packing?" Stafford wondered aloud as he fit it into his saddlebag.

"There's no telling how many days we'll be gone."

"They only have a day's jump on us, Jessie, and they have women and children," Stafford reasoned.

Jessie smiled. "Don't be fooled by that. If they're in a hurry they can cover twice as much ground as we can. They have more horses, and they wouldn't hesitate to push them till they dropped."

Stafford nodded his agreement. "Maybe we should get two more mounts ourselves."

"I was thinking of it, but it might cause suspicion and raise too many questions." Again the lieutenant nodded. "We'll have to make do with what we have," Jessie concluded.

"Then the sooner we get started the better," Stafford said as he mounted his horse.

Without a word Jessie swung up into her saddle and started down the trail.

★

Chapter 13

At first the sign was a little hard to find, there were so many sets of hoofprints. But Jessie followed Stafford's hunch, and a little north of the abandoned village she found a clearly marked trail. From there on in the sign was easy to follow. The marks the poles of the travois left were unmistakable. While both riders had been searching for the sign they had remained quiet, but now Stafford had something to ask.

"Jessie, what makes you so certain Ki is with the Comanches?"

"The last we knew he went up to speak with the Indians. Lucy Becker never saw him that night or next morning. Where else could he be?"

"Just wondering." Stafford seemed to be thinking things over. He started to speak several times, then changed his mind. Eventually he just spoke up. "Jessie, I have a confession to make," he began.

"About all those ladies in every frontier town," Jessie said with a smile.

"I never kiss and tell," he reported slyly. "I had two good reasons for coming along."

"Go ahead," Jessie urged him on.

"Well, when I took my commission, I took on a certain responsibility," he stated seriously. "One was to obey

rders, and the other was to protect the people. In my mind
t was never a problem which came first. Right now we
eckon Ki is held by hostiles. It's my duty to try and rescue
im. I don't need to worry about any orders. So you see,
'm not really concerned with the consequences of my ac-
ions. There's a clear and immediate danger here, not only
o Ki, but to you as well. I couldn't turn my back on that.
t'll stand in any court-martial proceeding."

"I'm glad you feel that way, Stafford. What's your other
eason?"

Stafford unhooked his saber from his belt and attached it
o his saddle. "It'll be more comfortable like that," he said
o no one in particular.

"You're avoiding the question, Lieutenant."

Stafford shook his head. "No, I just want to make sure
you won't take offense."

"Try me."

"Well, I got this sneaking suspicion that the other reason
I was so eager to come along was to spend another night
out here with you."

"Sounds reasonable. You're not the first good-looking
man who's followed me around just to get the chance to
hold me in his arms."

"That may be true, but I ain't talking about just holding
you," he said with a wink.

"Lieutenant!" Jessie scolded.

"Aw, Jessie, you're not mad again, are you?"

"You'll just have to find out later, won't you?" she said
with a wink of her own.

For the remainder of the day they rode in comparative
silence. A cold northern wind started to blow, and Jessie
wrapped her scarf around her face. Stafford also turned up
his collar. It was easier to refrain from talking than to have
to shout above the howling wind.

A combination of boredom and anxiety started to eat at
Jessie. She was tired of riding the same terrain. Though the
land was no longer flat, it still lacked any interesting fea-

tures. There were low ridges and rocky mounds, and everywhere a scattering of bare trees. Periodically there were a few cedars to lend some color to the drab landscape, but for the most part Jessie found every mile to be similar to the last. Jessie was also tired of fighting the weather. The wind blew unceasingly, and the combination of stinging cold and unrelenting gusts was slowly wearing Jessie down.

She started to think of Stafford, and how warm his body would feel next to hers. She began to picture his strong torso pressing against her, their legs intertwined. She knew that nestled against him she could find a brief respite from the cold. Though she was tempted to halt for the day, it would not serve her purpose. The cold and the boredom were only part of the picture. She had ridden the winter ranges of the Circle Star countless times till she thought she could recognize every bush, and she had been out in much colder climates than this. But she was never made as irritable by nature and the elements as this stretch of Indian Territory was now making her. She would have liked to have let Stafford soothe away her worries, but she was fully aware the major source of her concern would not vanish no matter how close Stafford held her. Not until she knew Ki was safe would she be able to relax totally. No matter how pleasant, she blocked all thoughts of Stafford from her mind. Jessie could not stop now. She knew there was no other choice but to go on.

But even with all Jessie's fortitude, there came a time when they had to stop for the night. They were looking for a suitable place when Stafford saw strangers approaching from the distant west. He started to alert Jessie, but she was already watching their approach.

"Any idea who they might be?" She reached into her jacket pocket and took hold of her Colt.

"They're not Indians, that much I can tell you."

It was also clear to Jessie that the approaching party

consisted of two riders and a man in a wagon. There was no other alternative but to wait and see.

The three strangers must have spotted them as well, for they now changed direction and headed straight for them. "Don't worry, Jessie. Doesn't look like trouble," Stafford assured her. Yet he slipped his Winchester from its boot and slung it across his lap.

"Shall we go out and meet them?" Jessie asked.

"They'll be here shortly. We can wait." There was a confidence in his tone that Jessie did not question.

The cavalry officer was right. In a very short time the wagon and riders had crossed the distance and were drawing up alongside Stafford's horse.

"Mr. Tyler," Stafford said with a bit of surprise.

"Good day, Lieutenant, ah . . . ?"

"Stafford."

"That's right, Stafford. It's a pleasant surprise to see you and your companion."

"Oh, excuse me, sir. This is Jessie Starbuck. Jessie, Mr. Tyler."

"Charlie Tyler, Department of the Interior?" Jessie asked.

The man in the wagon tipped his black bowler hat. "The very same. And you must be the Jessie Starbuck whose arrival we've been awaiting."

Jessie studied the man before answering. He was not what she had expected. He was small of frame and neatly dressed. With his wire-rimmed spectacles and beaver-trimmed wool coat he would have looked more in place in some Kansas City bank than out on the prairie in the middle of nowhere. But she was certain the man was not as meek as he appeared, and she would deal with him cautiously. "That's right," she answered his question. "I've been trying to see you since we got here. You haven't been in your office."

"Regrettably, I've been away on business. But now's as good a time as any," he said pleasantly. He climbed stiffly down from the wagon, then straightened and rebuttoned his long coat. Unlike a banker, Jessie noted the presence of a Colt Peacemaker strapped securely to his hip. "It's not my office, but we can make the best of it. We were just about to stop for the night. Why don't you join us?"

Jessie didn't answer. She had matters to discuss with Tyler, but she didn't wish to spend the night camped with others. She had different things in mind for her and Stafford. She looked to the lieutenant, hoping he would handle the situation gracefully. Tyler saw her hesitation and turned to the army officer. "Lieutenant, there's not much daylight left. You wouldn't get much farther. We have a slab of beef and a bottle of whiskey. . . ."

"That's a hard offer to pass up," Stafford said as he swung down from the saddle. "He's right, Jessie. We wouldn't make the next ridge before darkness was upon us." His tone was pleasant, but there was an apologetic look in his eyes.

"I understand," Jessie said, and she did. It would raise too many questions if they refused the man's hospitality. And questions were what they wanted to avoid.

"Good. Partridge'll start a fire, and we'll be eating in no time. Oh, pardon me, let me make proper introductions." He gestured as he named names. "This is Jake Partridge and his fellow farmer Bob Harrison, Lieutenant Stafford and Jessie Starbuck."

Jessie focused on Partridge. She would not have recognized him at first, but now could clearly make out the "farmer" who had brought the dead Indian into the fort. On closer inspection he looked no more a homesteader than he had the other day. She turned to Harrison. He had deep-set eyes and a strong jawline. Harrison seemed cut from the same cloth as Partridge. Jessie doubted if either one of them had ever stood behind a plow. But she didn't mention anything to that effect. Instead she turned back to study Tyler. A man could be judged by the company he keeps. What did this say about the agent for the Indian bureau?

She also noted that Tyler seemed to be in charge. He didn't suggest Partridge make a fire; he flat-out ordered it. There was much to learn here. Jessie felt that sixth sense flare up. The one that told you you were not alone in a dark room. The very same sense that woke you in the middle of the night when danger was near. Jessie looked at all three men. She knew she would have to tread lightly. She stole a fast look at Stafford. Did he too sense danger? From his demeanor there was no way of telling, but that was good. She hoped her words or actions did not bespeak her suspicions. Their very safety might depend on her ability to act innocent.

Though she would make no open accusations, she still wanted to confront Tyler and find out where he stood. She waited till after dinner. There was no reason to ruin a good meal, and besides, an opening presented itself as soon as they finished eating.

Tyler wiped his mouth with a kerchief he pulled from his pocket, and then he stretched out. "Not a bad cut of meat," he said happily.

"A sight better than the Comanches get to eat, Mr. Tyler."

"I haven't been invited to many Indian dinners, Miss Starbuck." His comment brought a chuckle from his two companions.

"Neither have I, but I've seen the rotting carcasses around the Indian village."

"That's easy enough to explain."

"Before you do," she interrupted, "I think you should know I know something about cattle myself."

"What a pleasing bit of modesty," Tyler said with an ingratiating smile. "As proprietor of the Circle Star ranch I would expect you to be rather informed on the subject."

"So I want straight answers," she said curtly. "Why do they get meat on the hoof?" she asked simply.

"It's the way they want it, Miss Starbuck. They weren't

141

happy receiving provisions of beef. We started that way, but they were suspicious."

"Of getting bad beef ?" she said sarcastically.

Tyler ignored the question and its pointed barb. "They are a hunting people," he explained further. "I imagine getting beef the way a child is given food offended their sensibilities."

There was some logic to that, but Jessie felt Tyler was avoiding the issue. "Either way, they're getting bad beef."

"Miss Starbuck, I'm hardly responsible for—"

"There's your name on the meat contract," Jessie accused openly. "Don't try to deny it. I've already had a talk with the drover."

"I didn't know that." Tyler let his surprise show.

"Why should you?"

"No reason, of course," he said amiably.

"Brunner also told me some other very interesting facts," Jessie added, deciding to press her advantage.

"Now I wish we *were* back in my office," Tyler said with a smile. "I don't actually arrange the contracts, Miss Starbuck. I just make sure they get carried out as agreed."

Jessie didn't really believe him, but there was no purpose in dwelling on the topic. She moved onward. "Then there's the question of infected blankets." She thought it curious that her accusation registered no surprise with the agent.

Tyler shrugged. "Again, there's the central purchasing office in Washington. I have no say in the matter. I'm here as an agent of the government to see the Indians get what's coming to them."

Jessie wondered at the true meaning behind his words. There were many different ideas as to what the Indians deserved, not all of them beneficial to red men.

Tyler continued. "Miss Starbuck, it's not easy appropriating money for the Indian reservations. Many people feel we should not be supporting them at all. We have to make do on the small budget we have. Granted, there are those who take advantage of that. We sometimes find ourselves dealing with men of, shall we say, less than high caliber. Merchants who slip in damaged goods not up to the letter of the contract."

"It's all very confusing, Mr. Tyler." Though Jessie was playing naive, there was some truth to her statement. Every time she thought she had the situation figured out, there was always something new that didn't fit. At first she thought the cattle drover was the answer to the diseased beef problem, but he turned out to be only a cog in the machine. Then when she thought Colonel McKenzie was behind the whole problem, Ki pointed out the one flaw in that argument, the homesteaders. Now when she sought to place the blame on Charlie Tyler, the Department of the Interior agent was calm and elusive.

"When you get back, drop in my office. I think we'll be able to clear up a few things," he said with a smile.

"I'll do just that," Jessie promised. There was no evidence to substantiate her feeling, but Jessie sensed Tyler's last comment was a bribe in the making. Corrupt men had tried to buy her off many times before, and she was very sensitive to that first subtle innuendo. That Tyler might be offering her a bribe did not bother her in the least. What might follow next did. In the past, when those who tried to buy her failed, often their next step was to try to silence her—permanently.

Jessie rose to her feet. "It's been a tiring day. If you don't mind, I think I'll turn in now."

Tyler stood up. "No, of course not. Sleep well, Miss Starbuck."

Jessie turned to Stafford. "Good night, Lieutenant."

There was regret in Stafford's eyes as he tipped his hat to her. "Night, Jessie."

Jessie nodded to the others, then rolled out her blanket on the far side of the fire. As she crawled into her bedroll she reckoned she'd sleep lightly at best. Her mind was still preoccupied with the situation at hand. Was it possible she was going too far trying to place the blame on any one individual? Could it be that no one person was exclusively at fault? Was everyone involved—including the Comanches—somewhat to blame? It would only take a little from each party to create an explosive atmosphere. As Ki once told her, no single snowflake feels responsible for the ensuing blizzard. Suddenly she cared little for the Comanches, the homesteaders, or the army. Ki was somewhere out there and Jessie's only concern now was getting him back.

She rolled over and told herself he was safe. She closed her eyes and slowly drifted off into a light sleep. But then visions of Stopher Dineen floated by, followed by Smith and Jones, the two cowboys who had tried to bushwhack them. Then finally she saw Yellow Deer's crying baby. She opened her eyes with a start. Someone was trying to kill the Comanche babies. Someone had also succeeded in murdering the whiskey smuggler. And there had already been one attempt against her life. Her head cleared instantly. These things did not happen of themselves. They were coldheartedly planned and executed. Jessie's hand slipped into her pocket. Her fingers curled around the smooth, polished peachwood handle of her Colt .38. She closed her eyes, though she knew she would not sleep a wink.

Stafford was up at the first sign of light. He started the fire and set a pot of water to boil. Jessie was packed and ready before the coffee was finished. They drank the hot, bitter brew in silence and were back on the trail before Tyler and his two friends woke up.

The sky was overcast, but even without the sun it promised to be a warmer day; there was no wind to speak of. As they rode Jessie and Stafford engaged in easy conversation. After spending a night almost as strangers, they were happy for the chance to talk freely to each other. It also was nice not to have to shout above the wind.

In the still morning air, they clearly heard the approach of the galloping horse. Jessie wheeled around to see the rider coming up on their rear. It looked to be Partridge, but Jessie couldn't be certain. This time they didn't wait for the rider, but turned their horses and met him halfway. Jessie was cautious, but it seemed any attack would have been done in a more secretive manner. The fact that they also outnumbered the lone rider two to one allowed Jessie to feel somewhat secure.

"Mornin'," Partridge hailed, as his horse slowed to a walk. "Charlie almost forgot to ask if you was intending to stop by any of the homesteads along the river."

"We might swing around back that way," Stafford informed him.

"Well, if you do, Charlie's calling a meeting of all the farmers this Sunday. If you can spread the word, we'd be much obliged."

"We'll do what we can," Jessie said.

"That's fine, ma'am. I'll be on my way, then." He turned his horse around and started to walk off.

Stafford and Jessie swung their horses around, then Jessie decided it might be a good idea to watch Partridge ride off into the distance. She turned in her saddle in time to see the man draw his sixgun.

"There's one other thing I forgot to say: Hands up!"

Even though she saw him make his move there was little Jessie could do. By the time Stafford turned around the gun was pointed right at Jessie. There was absolutely nothing he could have done. Jessie and Stafford both raised their hands over their heads. Partridge inched his horse over alongside Jessie's, the gun now at point-blank range. "Slide down nice an' easy, lady," Partridge ordered, then he turned to the lieutenant. "Throw down your gun, real slow." Stafford did as he was told. "Now the rifle. You put more'n two fingers around that stock an' I'll blow the lady's head off," he warned. Stafford moved with extreme caution. "Good." Partridge smiled confidently, then dismounted quickly to stand next to Jessie.

For a brief moment, Stafford thought he had a chance to throw himself at the gunman, but he checked his impulse at the last second. With the gun just a few inches from Jessie's temple, there was no margin for error. Stafford would have to sit tight and wait for a better opportunity.

"What do you want, mister?" Jessie asked boldly.

A slow smile crossed his lips. "I wouldn't be in no hurry to find out, missy."

"You lay a finger on her, Partridge, and I'll see you dead before the sun goes down," Stafford said threateningly. He didn't know exactly how he would carry out his promise, but at the moment the little details did not concern him.

"An' I'll see you slide down from yer saddle first. Nothing funny now, just nice an' easy. An' keep yer hands up." He waited till the lieutenant was standing on the ground before he turned back to Jessie. "Open yer jacket, and yer shirt."

"It's awfully cold, mister," Jessie protested softly.

"Do as I say," Partridge snapped. "And you," he addressed Stafford, "start walking thataway. I see your legs stop and she gets it."

Jessie had to think fast. She needed Stafford here to keep Partridge's attention divided. It would make it much harder if he was only concentrating on her. "Jake," she began in the sweetest voice she could muster, "looks like a girl could enjoy it with a man like you."

"Hear that, Lieutenant? Missy's gonna enjoy what I give her."

"Why shouldn't I, Jake? I could make it real nice for you. I could lay down and wrap my warm jacket around us both."

"Maybe you should stick around and watch this, Lieutenant," Partridge said with an ugly grin. "Get over there where I can keep an eye on you." Stafford moved around a

146

few yards behind Jessie. "Now, down on yer heels. Remember, you make a move and it'll be the end of her."

"I like a man that's forceful and strong," Jessie cooed.

"Get down on the ground, and take off yer pants."

Partridge was not wasting any more time, but that was fine with Jessie. The faster he moved the sooner she could get it over with. Still, Jessie hated to have to strip naked for the man. As she pulled down her pants she saw his eyes go wide with excitement. There'd be more than one surprise awaiting this Mr. Partridge, she told herself dryly.

With one hand Partridge ripped open his pants. His erect member sprung free. "I'll kill you, Partridge, you hear me?" Stafford shouted, though he made not the slightest move.

If only the gun weren't trained on Jessie, Stafford would willingly charge the man. He didn't care about his own safety, but as long as there was the chance Jessie could get shot, he would remain where he was, no matter how painful that might prove to be. But if the revolver wavered even slightly...

"Shut up an' watch," the gunman yelled back. "It may be the last thing you see in yer miserable life."

While the two men exchanged comments, Jessie took the opportunity to bring her legs together and wrap her jacket tighter around her.

"Open that jacket," Partridge snapped. "An' spread yer legs, missy." Desire oozed from his words.

Jessie spread her legs wide. Partridge was captivated by the sight. She slid her hands into her jacket pockets and pulled open her coat invitingly. "I think I'm going to like this, Jake," she said seductively. She lifted her hips slightly.

Jake's eyes glazed over, and his jaw dropped as he stared at Jessie's creamy white thighs. He moved closer, his eyes riveted to the center of her femininity.

"Come and get it, Jake," she whispered enticingly as she opened her thighs even wider.

He took another step, and three sharp explosions rang

147

out. Partridge's body spewed blood. Three holes in Jessie's coat pocket were smoking from the powder burns. And though it was hard to tell, there were three holes in Partridge's body as well. They were so close together, the bullets had slammed out a whole section of his chest. The area where his heart should have been was a growing stain of bright red. He toppled over backward, visions of Jessie's soft curly mound still in his head as he passed through the gates of hell.

They left the body for the wolves or the buzzards, whichever claimed it first, then continued on the trail of the Comanches. There was a brief moment when they considered going after Tyler, but Jessie reasoned the agent could wait. They would get him later. Ki, on the other hand, might be in need of immediate assistance.

Later in the afternoon the wind began to blow again, but this time it brought with it large white snowflakes. At first the shimmering white crystals danced gently around them, but then as the wind picked up, the few flakes turned into a solid sheet of stinging cold frost.

"We're heading into a bad storm, Jessie," Stafford shouted above the howling winds.

Jessie looked into the blackening sky. "Can we make a run for it?" she shouted back. Sometimes it was possible to outrun a storm—if, of course, you had somewhere to run to.

Stafford shook his head. "We're miles from the nearest homestead, and I'm not even sure which way. But we'll have to find shelter somewhere."

The high winds were making it almost impossible to hear, but Jessie got the gist of his words. She studied the terrain for a suitable shelter. There was no rocky ledge or outcropping in sight. Save for a few small trees and saplings, the land was flat and barren. "It looks like what Partridge couldn't take care of, Mother Nature will," Jessie said, though she doubted Stafford could hear her.

★

Chapter 14

The Comanches marched nonstop. Ki was amazed by the fortitude of these people. Old men and young children endured mile after mile without the slightest complaint. Even the beasts of burden held up under the strain. All day, through the night, and into the next day they pushed forward. Periodically a family would rest by the wayside, but only long enough to feed or change horses. Then they continued on to rejoin the rear of the column.

As Running Wolf's family passed other Indians, or as they were passed in turn, Ki tried to spot his nocturnal visitor. Many young squaws returned his stares, but it was more a look of curiosity than intimacy. Ki wanted to believe he would intuitively recognize the woman, knowing her instantly at first glance, but he knew it was unlikely. He wondered if he would see her again one night once they had arrived at their destination. The thought darkened his mood. Would the Comanches ever reach their destination? It was probable that Ki would never know the identity of his female friend, but he realized that was no reason not to repay her kindness and trust. The best way to show his gratitude would be to help her people. He had to find a way to make the Comanches see reason. Though he devoted his full concentration to that issue, every step across the cold prairie took him no closer to an answer.

He was pulled from his thoughts by the cold, stinging snowflakes whipping across his face. The sky was dark and the snow was falling fast. Ki expected the Indians to stop and set up camp. He understood the Comanches' urgent need to put as much distance as possible between themselves and the soldiers at Fort Butler, but judging by the increasing velocity of the wind the storm looked like it would prove severe. It would not only prohibit pursuit by the cavalry, it would make finding shelter a necessity. He didn't think it would take any more time to set up the village than it had to tear it down. He already knew that with a small fire the tepees would provide ample warmth, and he was almost as certain they would stand up to the high winds. Therefore, he was very surprised to find the Indians continuing their trek.

Ki began to notice young braves and older children darting off in all directions, leather pouches in their hands. He wondered why, till he saw a small boy in front of him bend down and pick up a large buffalo chip. If there was considerable snow accumulation, finding wood—especially dry wood—would be difficult. The dry and hardened buffalo droppings would burn slowly and give off high heat.

He turned to Yellow Deer. "Give me a pouch and I will help." The Comanche woman looked at him with distrust. "Where would I run to, Yellow Deer?" he said in answer to her unasked question. "I will be warmed by the fires too. Let me do my share," he pleaded sincerely. Reluctantly she handed him a sack, and Ki trotted off in search of the fuel.

It took Ki longer than he had expected to fill the bag. The buffalo chips were hard to spot, but soon Ki got the knack of differentiating the flat, gray-brown disks from the rocky, brown-gray dirt. When he returned to the line of marching Indians he saw the backs of men and beasts alike were covered with blankets of white snow. And still they continued to plow through the storm.

Because of the low visibility and the fact that Ki was

walking with his head down into the wind, the mountainous ridge seemed to spring up out of nowhere. Soon they were picking their way up a rocky slope. Ki couldn't see the top, but he suspected the range was not too high—though from the route they were following it was hard to tell. There were countless switchbacks, and every time Ki thought they had come to the summit, he saw it was just a ridge leveling off temporarily. One thing was obvious; the Comanche leaders were familiar with the land and knew exactly where they were going, otherwise it would have been impossible to find or follow the rocky mountain pass.

After cutting from one ridge to the next, the trail began to descend steeply. It then became clear why the Comanches did not stop to set up camp on the plain. Here, stretched out below them, was a quiet, sheltered basin nestled nicely between the mountains. A strip of bottomland against the north wall was so protected it was totally bare of snow.

By the time they made it down to the basin floor the first tepees were already set up. The lodgings were arranged closer together than on the reservation, since they all sought out dry land and squeezed close against the shelter of the north wall. Ki was struck by how quiet it was—how nearly silent. There was virtually no wind in the basin, and as a result it was considerably warmer. When they pulled up alongside the last tepee, Ki offered to help Yellow Deer assemble the tent, but she refused. Ki did not insist. As he watched Yellow Deer and two other squaws erect the tepee, he realized he would have just been in the way.

Once they entered the tepee Ki was glad he had helped gather buffalo chips. The animal droppings caught fire quickly, and soon the interior of the tepee was warm and cozy. Ki didn't realize how cold he was till he shed his heavy jacket and the warmth of the fire began to soothe his tired body. As they spread out the thick buffalo hides and settled down around the fire, Ki began to feel more like one of the family than a prisoner of the Indians.

Just then Running Wolf entered. He had been traveling at the front of the column, and now Ki assumed he had come to rejoin his family and relax. But the Comanche leader did not sit down. He pointed his finger at Ki. "Come, Spirit HalfBreed," he commanded.

Ki rose to his feet, then reached down to grab his jacket. "Will I need this?" he asked.

"It does not matter," the Indian answered curtly.

Ki wondered at that. Although there were no ominous tones in the Comanche's voice, Ki did not like the subtle implication inherent in the answer. He took the coat with him. In a fight the garment would be hindrance, but if Ki found himself exposed to the elements for any length of time the jacket would provide warmth. Reluctantly, he followed Running Wolf outside.

The Indian led him behind the row of tepees to the rear corner of the basin. There they followed a narrow footpath a third of the way up the slope. They inched around a large boulder, then Running Wolf dropped to his knees and disappeared into a narrow opening in the rock wall. Ki followed on hands and knees.

As soon as he stuck his head into the tunnel, warm air hit his face. If there were hot springs running somewhere through the mountain, the basin would prove to be an even more ideal winter camp than Ki had at first realized. Then Ki heard a faint, eerie drone coming from deep within the passage. He didn't think it was the natural sound of wind rushing among the rocks, but it ended before he could identify the source.

"You can stand up now, Spirit HalfBreed." The darkness was so intense Ki could not see the Comanche. Though he did not doubt Running Wolf's words, he rose to his feet slowly, half-expecting to bump his head against the rock. "This way," the voice urged him on.

Ki brushed against the wall and had to feel with his

ands to make it past a curve in the passageway. As he urned the corner, a soft light filtered through the darkness f the tunnel. Ki could make out his Indian guide a few teps ahead of him. Then they turned another corner and ne cavern was ablaze with light.

The tunnel opened up into a large, high-ceilinged natural cavern. Ki now saw the source of the mysterious sound. The elders of the tribe, naked from the waist up, sat around huge bonfire and began another chant. A drum beat a low, steady rhythm.

As Ki approached the gathering, Black Elk reached for is lance. Ki stiffened; had he been brought here for a eremonial execution? Had the Comanche leaders already decided his fate? But why had they gone to the trouble? If hey had planned to kill him, why didn't they do it back on he reservation? What had he done, or what had transpired luring their journey that might have swayed their minds? His eyes darted around quickly for a means of escape, but as he glanced at the Indians to note their number and positions something did not seem right. Their faces, especially he chief's, did not have the steely countenance he would have expected with a sentence of death. On the contrary, Black Elk's expression seemed warm and friendly. Ki, hough, did not allow himself to relax. He was not familiar with their ways and should not try to read anything in their faces or the situation. He was a foreigner among natives, possibly hostile ones.

Without warning Black Elk sent the spear flying toward Ki. It landed in the dirt, just inches from Ki's foot.

"Take my lance, Spirit HalfBreed. Join our circle."

"That way," Stafford shouted loudly. He pointed to the stand of trees, the only thing in sight that might offer any shelter.

The grove wasn't tightly planted and the trees weren't big enough to provide satisfactory protection, but Jessie didn't mention that. What alternative did they have? As

153

they got a few yards from the trees, the answer provided itself: a buffalo wallow. Jessie and Stafford noticed it simultaneously. The shallow, round depression was big for a wallow, but small for a gully, and might prove just the right size.

"Try and stake your horse down," Stafford said. "I'll be back soon," he shouted as he galloped over to the trees. He pulled a rope from his saddlebag, dismounted, then tied one end of the rope around the trunk of a young cedar. The other end he tied around his saddlehorn. He swung back into the saddle and kicked his horse forward. Jessie, rope in hand, now drew her mount alongside his. "I thought I told you to get into that wallow."

"You did. But I think this is more important." Without another word she smoothly lassoed the top of another sapling. Stafford marveled at her expertise with a rope, though at any other time his pride might have been injured.

They dragged the two trees over to the wallow and laid them across the top. "See if you can get that other sapling. I'll try and cut some branches," he said as he drew his saber.

The last of the saplings proved to be a bit tougher to uproot than the others, but with Stafford pushing his weight against the base of the trunk, it soon toppled. As Jessie dragged it over to the others, Stafford went on to attack the branches of the larger trees.

He hacked away at the low branches with a muscle born of desperation. A few whacks was all it took to break all the branches within reach. He started to drag them over when Jessie took the limbs from his hands. "You keep cutting. I'll take care of these." Stafford nodded and went back to the tree. He realized then that he had made a slight mistake. By chopping the low branches first the upper ones were now out of reach. But when he climbed into his saddle and stood in the stirrups, he was able to cut a few more branches. Jessie dragged these away, and Stafford began attacking the last tree from the top down.

154

It became progressively harder to tackle each branch. The icy winds were taking their toll. Even with his leather gloves, Stafford found it hard to maintain a firm grip on his saber. Each impact of metal against wood sent a painful sting through his swollen, frozen hands. When he started on the lower branches he discarded his sword altogether and used his foot instead to crack the boughs. He was almost finished before he started to wonder where Jessie was. She had not returned in quite some time. A twinge of fear shot through him. Was she all right? Had she collapsed in the cold? He fought the impulse to drop what he was doing and search for her. If he didn't finish what he was doing neither of them would survive. Regardless of what happened to her she could not have strayed far. The best thing would be to get the shelter set up, then go and find her. But his anxiety won over his reason. He went racing back to the wallow.

"Jessie, Jessie," he shouted, though his voice couldn't be heard more than a few feet away. The wind stung his eyes and tears formed, causing his vision to blur. In his panic he almost ran past the buffalo wallow. The depression, transformed into a low dome of piled branches, was covered with a layer of snow and blended in with the rest of the flat, white landscape. Stafford called out again, but Jessie was nowhere to be seen. He turned suddenly and almost bumped into her. She carried a good-sized rock in her arms. "I thought you were, I was afraid . . .'"

"I'm all right," Jessie assured him. "Let's get inside."

"One more trip . . ." he answered and took off for the last of the branches. It took him two more trips, the final one with saddle in hand, before he was able to crawl into the shelter.

Once inside the den he could see that Jessie had been busy herself. The depression was actually more egg-shaped than round, and though the dome of branches formed a good roof, it only met the ground to form a wall on three sides. Jessie had gathered rocks and piled them up to fill the gap. She used her saddle for a makeshift door. There wasn't enough headroom for Stafford to sit up comfortably, but there was plenty of space for him to stretch his legs fully. He lay back on the blanket Jessie had spread across the ground.

"I never even saw you take the bedrolls. Where's the other one?" he asked curiously.

Jessie pointed above their heads. "It's part of the roof. I wanted to make sure we'd stay dry."

"Good idea. It'd be hard staying warm if snow kept seeping in on us."

"I also scraped out the snow in here. I didn't think lying on melted snow would be too comfortable."

Stafford looked around appreciatively. "All we need is a small fire, and we'd have all the comforts of home."

"I'd be worried about the branches catching fire," Jessie replied.

"More importantly, we have to make sure enough snow falls and freezes on us. Once the roof is solid we might try a small fire."

Jessie understood. The snow itself would provide the best insulation against the cold. If a fire kept the roof warm enough to melt the snow they would be much worse off. "We'll have to find some other way of getting warm."

"There's only one way I can think of," Stafford said with a smile.

"Me, too," Jessie agreed. She was already removing her jacket.

"Jessie, I was just teasing," Stafford exclaimed. "You'll freeze."

"I think we'll both freeze if we don't."

"Are you serious?"

"Dead serious. Now off with your clothes. Doctor's orders."

Stafford removed his boots reluctantly. "You know, ordinarily you wouldn't have to ask twice."

Jessie leaned forward and pressed her lips against his.

156

While her tongue danced with his, her hand unbuttoned her shirt. Her nipples sprung out fully erect. "If I don't feel your warm body against me soon, Lieutenant, I think I *will* freeze," she said with a shudder.

Stafford pulled off his jacket, then rolled to his side and removed his pants quickly. Jessie, now naked herself, was pulling off his shirt. As soon as his hands were free, he pulled Jessie tightly against his body and placed his mouth over hers. Jessie reached behind her and pulled her jacket up around them.

"I wish I could see your eyes now, Jessie. Seems like it's always pitch-black every time I hold you like this. And in here there won't even be any moonlight."

"I wish I could see you too, Stafford, but at least I can feel you," she answered, as she ran her fingers up his muscular thigh.

Stafford responded in kind and began stroking the inside of her soft thighs. "Touching you makes me want to see you even more. I know you're a beautiful woman, Jessie. I'd love to feast my eyes on every inch of you."

"Your fingers are doing a good job of that." Her breath was becoming heavy, as his fingers traced a pattern all over her body. "I think I'm feeling warm already," Jessie said softly. She took hold of his hard rod.

"That's not warm you're feeling, Jessie, that's my—" Jessie ran her tongue softly across Stafford's lips before he could finish his sentence. As her tongue played with his lips, his fingers parted hers. She gasped as a finger slid slowly into her. Unconsciously, she started to stroke Stafford's rigid tool, at the same pace his finger probed into her.

Jessie no longer felt warm. She was hot, hot with desire. She wanted what was in her hand deep inside of her. As if Stafford read her mind, he slowly pulled his finger from her moist folds. Jessie let out a sigh of disappointment, which was then followed by a gasp of enjoyment as Stafford slowly replaced his finger with his large digit.

157

Jessie abandoned herself to the feeling and rocked her hips back and forth quickly. Stafford met her with powerful thrusts of his own. "I know I promised you we would go slow this time, but I can't help myself, Stafford." Of its own accord her muscles began gripping his shaft.

"And I promised you a warm fire," he replied with a smile. "If you don't hold me to that I won't hold you to your promise."

"But we have all night and more."

Stafford was not listening. He began to rock his body from side to side. Jessie felt her desire building up feverishly from deep within her. When Stafford's mouth found her breasts and sucked her hard bud into his mouth, she let out a small scream. That urged him on further, and he drove deeply into her.

Jessie couldn't tell which came first, the scream or the spasm that took hold of her body. But each thrust of Stafford's powerful body sent another tremor through her body and forced another scream from her lungs. It seemed to end only as she felt Stafford let loose with his own warm juice.

She didn't know how long it took her to recover. But when she caught her breath and her head stopped spinning, Stafford was resting quietly on top of her. She was warm and cozy, and all fears of freezing to death had vanished totally. There was a peaceful feeling in her soul. She didn't know if they would survive the storm, but listening to Stafford's soft breathing and the muted howling of the wind outside, she realized there were worse ways to meet your worldly end. In the past she had been driven by unfinished deeds, and felt her time could not come till she had achieved her goals. But now that the cartel was destroyed, a major objective of her life had been fulfilled. Ki had taught her there was an end to everything, but that an end was also a beginning. Closing her eyes, she wondered if anyone was ever ready to face that crossover. She would have liked to have said good-bye to Ki, to have known that he was safe. She felt a warm tear run down her cheek.

Stafford stirred, then lifted his head. She felt him kiss away her tears. "What's the matter, Jessie?" he asked softly. How could she possibly explain? She shook her head and remained silent.

"It's going to be all right," he whispered softly. She nodded her head. Stafford kissed her neck gently. "We'll get out of here. Don't worry."

"I know." She felt something stir within her, then realized it was Stafford growing hard and erect. They had never pulled apart; he had never slipped away. He started to rock slowly on top of her.

"I don't know how long the storm will blow. We'll have to try and keep our warmth up," he explained pragmatically.

"With all the heat we've generated so far, I'm surprised the roof hasn't melted on us."

"We'll have to go slow and be careful," he warned, as he continued to rock slowly on top of her.

Jessie spread her legs, and smiled. *Everything would be all right.* Even in one's wildest fantasies, it would never end like this. She rolled over on top of Stafford and kissed him passionately.

Chapter 15

The heat from the fire was intense. Ki now understood why it was not necessary for him to bring a jacket. Had he come without his coat, the chill from the few minutes of exposure would have been quickly chased away by the large bonfire. He saw a tall pile of wood off in the corner of the cavern. Judging from the size of the stockpile the Comanches had been here before and were well prepared. Ki removed his jacket and placed it under him before sitting down cross-legged.

Chief Black Elk began to talk in his native tongue; he seemed to be addressing the fire. Running Wolf, who sat beside Ki, leaned over and whispered in his ear. "He speaks to Father Peyote and asks him to share his gifts with you. He says you are a good man whose spirit is trained in the way but still walks the earth searching."

Ki looked at him with surprise. The "way" was the word that described Ki's spiritual and martial training. Few Westerners had ever heard the term, and Ki almost never spoke it himself. How then did this elderly Comanche come to use it, and correctly at that? He wanted to ask that of Running Wolf, but instead simply whispered back a one-word inquiry, "Why?"

"Black Elk has had a vision. It can't be denied," came the cryptic response.

Ki didn't expect any more of an explanation, so he turned his attention back to the Comanche chief. Black Elk removed a small pouch that hung around his neck. He rubbed it against his heart, then poured some of the contents into his hand. They looked like small brown buttons, no more than an inch in diameter. He held them in his hand, offered them to the fire, and made a short recitation before popping them in his mouth. After a few vigorous chews he spit the pulp back into his hand and again offered it to the fire. After replacing the paste back into his mouth he rubbed his palm all over his head, face, and chest. After a few more chews Ki saw Black Elk swallow deeply. The Comanche closed his eyes and began a soft chant. With his eyes still closed, he passed the pouch to his right, where the medicine man repeated the process. In addition, the medicine man reached to his side and threw a pile of sagebrush and other dried herbs onto the fire. They crackled loudly, their blue-gray smoke curling to the ceiling and filling the cavern with a sweet, pungent aroma.

The soft hide pouch was passed around till it finally came to Ki. He pulled out one of the buttons. Running Wolf took the purse from him and placed three more of the brown peyote buttons into Ki's hand. They were dry, hard, and ugly. As Ki placed them in his mouth he was reminded of the dried *shitake* mushrooms of his native land. But the analogy ended as he began to chew on the fuzzy buttons. They were very bitter, almost foul-tasting, and were made even more unpleasant by their dry, mealy texture. It took a lot of work, and saliva, to soften them to a paste. It was with great relief that he spit the pulp into his palm.

"Father Peyote, share your gift with me. Let me become one of your sons," he said aloud as he stretched his hand toward the fire. Out of the corner of his eye he could see Running Wolf nod with approval. He placed the pulp in his mouth. What he thought to himself was, "Father Peyote, let me swallow this vile mash and not get sick to my stomach." Surprisingly, he found his wish had been answered.

161

The peyote now tasted like chewed fruit rind, and he swallowed it without trouble.

Ki relaxed and became absorbed in the chanting. Each Indian seemed to be singing independently, yet all their voices blended together into one big vocal tapestry. Ki began to get the vague sense that time was distorting. Sometimes a single note would reverberate indefinitely, and then a lengthy passage would rush by and seem to last for only the briefest moment.

As he listened to the music, he felt like he was being carried along on the crest of a wave. Then, suddenly, he was tossed head over heels. His insides thrashed about and took hold of him. The first wave of nausea swept over him. His stomach began to convulse violently. There was no controlling it. Helpless, Ki pitched over and heaved the contents of his near-empty stomach into the dirt beside him. Another spasm racked his body, and then as quickly as it had come upon him, it was gone. His body was silent, his blurry vision cleared. He lay down, weak and exhausted. His back pressed against the warm earth, his eyes stared peacefully up into space. And the cavern ceiling glistened to life.

The gypsum in the rock glimmered like a thousand stars, while other minerals reflected the firelight and sparkled like gold and silver. Ki was reminded of the Golden Temple of Kyoto. The thought transported him back to his homeland. He saw peasants working the fields and proud samurai strutting about, their swords prominently displayed. There were bejeweled lords wearing rich clothes of silk, and shaven-headed monks in simple robes of yellow. But he not only saw all this, he smelled it, tasted it, and felt it.

But then visions of Jessie, her tawny mane blowing in the breeze, floated into his consciousness, and he realized the past was no more. The land of his childhood, thousands of miles away, might just as well have never existed, except in his memory. The West was the present, the every-

162

thing. As if to confirm this, herds of cattle stampeded across the plains in his mind. Ki could taste the dust in his mouth, then could feel the cool waters of a rushing stream wash away the grime. There were the hundreds of miles traveled on horseback, stagecoach, and rail, Jessie always at his side. He had left one world for another. The present consisted of boots, spurs, and sixguns. The past was sandals, sashes, and swords. His *katana*, or long sword, would be as effective against modern rifles as the Indian lance was against the high-powered Springfields. Sudden realization hit Ki.

For him it had been a relatively simple matter to give up his old world. A long ocean voyage had impressed upon him the necessity of leaving his old world behind. But the Indians had taken no such journey. They roamed the same lands that their fathers and their great-grandfathers' fathers before them had. They followed the same way of life, unchanged for hundreds of years. They had not recognized the coming of the white man as the coming of a new world, but it was. Civilization, with its towns, railroads, farms, and fenced grazing lands had transformed the Indians' land totally. With the coming of the white man the Indian way of life would never again be the same.

Ki started to hum a traditional Japanese song of mourning. He could visualize the courtesan sitting under a cherry tree, strumming her *koto*, pink blossoms falling gently around her. It was with a start that he opened his eyes and saw the Comanches staring at him. They had stopped their own chanting and were listening to him with interest. A slow smile crossed his face as he realized his mistake. The land where he was born was thousands of miles away, but his Japanese heritage was still a strong part of him. He could isolate his memories, but he could never pull out that part of him that was Oriental. Though he was living in a new world, the old world was very much with him. He thought again of his analogy of the *katana*. It was true that his samurai weapon was out of date here in the modern

West. But how about his *shuriken?* Ki couldn't count all the times he had relied on them to save Jessie's life or his own. One needn't abandon all the old ways. Some would always be useful; others should always be cherished. But in the end it was imperative to adapt to the world around you, no matter how strange or different.

"I have had a vision," Ki announced clearly.

"We are listening, Spirit HalfBreed," Black Elk said.

Ki wasn't sure how he could explain all his thoughts to the Indians, but he had to try. "I am of the people," he began. "My people are *numinu*. I am *numinu*, though I come from a great distance away. My people are very old. The song I have sung existed long before there were horses roaming these lands." The old chief nodded. They had tales of the time when the horse was unknown and the Comanches traveled on foot. "It is that old," continued Ki, "yet it exists in my soul, fresh as the morning dew."

He continued by explaining to them the need to stop fighting change. The white man could not be destroyed; but neither could the Comanche. "The Japanese in me lives, yet I walk in the white man's society. I preserve the ways of the *numinu*, the ways of my people," he concluded finally.

He studied the Indian faces and saw doubt and disbelief, but knew they were willing to be convinced. "I will prove to you I am *numinu*. What aspects of your life do you cherish most? What do you value above all else?"

Running Wolf translated the last of his words to make certain they all understood. A brief discussion ensued before Black Elk spoke. "Among all Indians the *numinu* are known for their horses. There is none who rides like a Comanche."

"I, too, know of your prowess, and though I could say I am your equal, I could not prove it to you here and now," Ki replied.

The Indians exchanged a few more words among themselves, then a few of them nodded in approval. Running

Wolf and another man got up and ran from the cavern. Black Elk turned to Ki. "There is something else the Comanche must be. As his father was, the son will be; so it has always been. There is none our equal. The *numinu* are great archers."

Ki smiled to himself. He was hoping they would choose archery as the test. Ki was an excellent bowman, trained from his youth. He had studied archery not only as a martial art, but as a spiritual discipline. He still kept current at his practice; there was a beautiful lacquered longbow back at the Circle Star.

Running Wolf returned shortly carrying two bows and two quivers. The Comanche handed one of each to Ki. The bow, of polished hickory, was about three feet in length. That was shorter than what Ki was used to, but the pull on the string seemed sufficiently tight. Ki now turned his attention to the arrows. The secret to accurate shooting lay in the arrows. Any deformity or irregularity would not only affect the flight of the projectile, but would make consistent shooting impossible. For maximum accuracy each arrow had to be an almost exact duplication of the others. He picked up an arrow and sighted down the shaft as he rotated it slowly. Then he studied the feathers; all three were of equal size, and were equally placed around the circumference of the shaft. All in all, they were superbly made. Even if he had never seen a Comanche shoot an arrow, he would have known just by looking at their craftsmanship that they were excellent archers.

"A white man never studies the bow and arrow so," Running Wolf commented.

Was Running Wolf now referring to Ki as a white man, or was he making the distinction between Ki and the whites? Ki was not sure how to take the remark, so he remained silent.

"I think maybe you do know something about the bow," Running Wolf added with a smile.

While Ki was familiarizing himself with the weapon,

the second Indian returned with two sacks and some rope. He filled the bag with dirt, then strung them up between two stalagmites.

Black Elk and Running Wolf had a brief exchange. The younger warrior explained, "First you will hit the bag, Spirit HalfBreed, then we shall see."

The sack hung thirty yards away in the dark recess of the cavern. Ki could barely make out the outline of the bag, but even the faintest image would suffice. He would aim the arrow with his inner eye, seeing his target in his mind, not in real space. Ki would have liked to test the bow once, but he feared such a request would be viewed as a weakness. He picked up his bow, nocked the arrow, and pulled the bowstring back to his ear. He steadied his body with deep breaths, then reduced his breathing to shallow inhalations. When it seemed he was no longer breathing, he uncurled his fingers. The arrow went speeding to its target, but sailed inches over the back. Ki knew instantly why he failed to hit his mark. "The wood has much spring to it. It gives more power than I expected," he remarked calmly. It was not said as an excuse, but rather as a simple observation.

"I give you one of my best bows, Spirit HalfBreed," Running Wolf informed him.

Again Ki could not be sure if the Comanche was offering a challenge or being supportive. "I will do it honor, Running Wolf," Ki answered as he nocked his next arrow.

Though he had missed with his first shot, he had handled the bow with skill, and Black Elk gave an encouraging comment. "Even the Comanche do not hit with every arrow," he announced.

Ki was pleased to know where the elderly chief stood, but it would make little difference. With or without support, Ki had no doubt where the next arrow would wind up. He raised the bow and focused his mind. The bow and arrow were no longer separate objects that he held in his hand, they were extensions of himself. It would not be the

166

arrow that would hit its mark; his very being would pierce the target. His eyes closed as he "saw" the target. The arrow charged through the air, then, still accelerating, it broke in two as it hit the rock wall.

For a moment the Indians looked dazed. Running Wolf was the first to the react and run to the target. He placed his hand under the bag. A thin stream of dirt trickled into his palm. The Comanche who had tied the sacks also went to investigate. Excitedly, he placed his finger into a hole that was in the dead center of the bag. A moment later he placed his other finger into a matching hole in the rear of the bag. The arrow had gone clear through.

"You shoot a mighty arrow," Running Wolf said with a smile as he walked back to rejoin Ki. "But now we test your skill." Was there the slightest trace of a wink, or was Ki just imagining that?

Running Wolf issued instructions to his fellow brave. The Indian went over to the second bag, untied one end of the rope, and started to swing it. The bag jerked erratically. Running Wolf slung the quiver of arrows over his shoulder and readied his bow. The muscles of his back stood out taut and hard as he pulled back the bowstring. The Comanche aimed and fired quickly. Before the first arrow reached its destination the second arrow was on its way. Before he had finished, Running Wolf had let fly four arrows. Despite the difficult moving target, they all hit their mark.

"You are very skilled," Ki said with sincere admiration. He too slung his quiver over his shoulder. He not only had to match the Comanche's aim, but his speed as well. Then Ki realized matching the Comanche tit for tat would not serve his purpose. He had to outdo him. It would not be an easy task; Running Wolf's shooting had been impressive.

Ki's target was already in movement. He raised his bow. Unlike Running Wolf's, Ki's muscles seemed fluid and re-laxed, though he drew back the bow as far as the Indian had. As he sighted down the shaft of the arrow, it came to him.

The arrow was no doubt a hunting one. Not only would a war arrow be too valuable to waste in such a contest, but with the near-extinction of the buffalo, the hunting arrows were now even less important. There were two major differences between the two types of arrows. First, the war arrow would be barbed; any attempt to remove the arrow would cause further ripping and tearing of flesh. The hunting arrow would be flat to facilitate its removal and reuse. The other difference, the position of the points, was even more important. The war arrow's point would be horizontal to fit between ribs of a man. Following the same principle, the large metal arrowhead on the hunting shaft would be vertical, and perpendicular to the ground, to pass between the ribs of a buffalo and pierce its vital organs.

But the vertical blade at the end of Ki's arrow would serve another purpose. He knew he was taking a gamble. If he succeeded the contest would be over; if he failed it would also come to an end. It was all or nothing. Ki focused on his target, then relaxed. He made sure he "saw" the results of his shot before he even loosed the first arrow. When he was satisfied, he fired two arrows quickly, though not as quickly as he could have, and not as quickly as his Indian counterpart. If he hit, a fraction of a second would matter little.

Suddenly the Indians burst out into raucous laughter; a few let out jubilant whoops. Amazed, Ki refocused his eyes. How could he have missed? Then a smile came to his face. The Comanches were not choosing sides and cheering for a victorious Running Wolf. They were celebrating skill and showmanship. With their cheers Ki knew he was accepted as one of them. The sack lay on the floor, the two arrows having sliced cleanly through the ropes on either side.

Running Wolf was laughing too. The Comanches were known to have a playful sense of humor, but until now Ki had not seen it. As was often the case, humor was reserved for members of the club.

Only Black Elk was not laughing. He held up his hand solemnly. Slowly the other Indians quieted down. "We will sit again around the fire and consult Father Peyote. Then we will speak," he said gravely.

This time the peyote experience was easier and more enjoyable. The taste bothered Ki less, and though he became nauseous again, he was prepared for it and it passed quickly. He sat relaxed and let visions of his squaw lover fill his mind, body, and soul. Though it had been dark when she visited, he clearly saw every feature of her face and figure. It was most pleasurable.

He was roused from his euphoria by Black Elk's deep voice. "I will tell you of my vision now, Spirit HalfBreed." All eyes turned toward the chief. "I see the plains, the very same lands the mighty buffalo roamed. But the great provider is gone. In its place I see another beast, one with a short coat and horns that curl out from the sides of its head. Horns that span more distance than a man can reach. These beasts graze happily, and all the while a brilliant bronze sun shines over them all."

"I share your vision, Black Elk. It is a vision of the future, one that will save your people." The answer was so simple he wondered why he or Jessie had not thought of it sooner. The beast of the chief's vision was clearly a Texas longhorn. Ki could have explained more, but he felt that Jessie would do a better job of it. "Your vision and my vision together are powerful medicine. You must come with me back to the reservation. We must talk to Jessie."

"Hair Like Setting Sun," Running Wolf added in clarification, using the Comanche-given name for Jessie.

It hit Ki and Black Elk simultaneously; symbolically, Jessie was represented in the chief's vision. The prophetic nature of the vision amazed Ki. He was thinking of what to say next to convince the Comanches when Black Elk rose to his feet.

He addressed the others in Comanche as he moved face-to-face with Ki. All eyes were on them. "There has long been a legend among our people that one day a great archer would come to lead us." Black Elk removed his feathered headband and placed it upon Ki's head.

★

Chapter 16

The storm ended sometime in the night. When Jessie and Stafford burrowed out from their snow lodge, the sun was shining brightly over a solid white landscape. After the comforting darkness of their den, Jessie had to shade her eyes from the blinding glare. "Do you see our horses?" was her first question.

"I can't see a thing," Stafford replied. He was also temporarily blinded, but his eyes adjusted quickly. "Wait, over there." He pointed to the stand of trees, where one of the horses was busy gnawing away at the bark of a cedar.

"Where's my horse?" Jessie wondered aloud. As they trudged through the knee-high snow they soon stumbled across the answer. The sorrell was half-buried under a snowdrift, frozen solid. "I was afraid this would happen," she said sadly.

"There was nothing you could have done, Jessie," Stafford said as he placed a comforting arm around her. "We're lucky we still have the one horse. I'll saddle her and we'll be on our way."

It took a minute to decide their next course of action. Neither Jessie nor Stafford wanted to turn back, but the snow had wiped out all traces of sign and made their continued pursuit of the Comanches difficult at best.

"I reckon the Comanches hit the storm same as us. They had to hole up, too," Stafford said as he tightened the cinch on the saddle. "We got as good a chance as any to pick up their trail farther on. We'll catch 'em eventually," he added encouragingly.

"But how far can we go in a day with one horse?" She already knew the answer to her question. Doubling up on the horse would tax not only the animal but the riders as well.

"We can always turn back," Stafford suggested, though he didn't seemed enthused at the prospect. "But Ki's still out there somewhere," he added as if to sway her mind.

"I hardly need reminding," she shot back quickly. Then she softened her tone. "Believe me, Stafford, I haven't forgotten."

"There's no second-guessing a Comanche," he said almost to himself. "Why don't we head west? Either we'll pick up some sign or, if not, we'll hit one of the homesteads. We'll get you another mount, then swing back north. . . ."

"Sounds good. You want to walk or ride first shift?" she asked jokingly.

But Stafford was already sitting high in the saddle. He responded by leaning down, grabbing her around her waist, and sweeping her up off her feet. Jessie willingly assisted his efforts with a helpful hop. It was a tight yet comfortable fit between the saddlehorn and the Lieutenant's body. "That answer your question, Miss Starbuck?" Stafford said as he nudged the horse forward.

They headed straight for the mountains. The other day the low mountain range had been totally obscured by the gray, overcast sky, but today the bright sun caused the snow-covered peaks to twinkle like a brilliant-cut diamond.

Before long they saw a small homesteader's shack in the distance. "It's ironic how close we were to shelter," Jessie remarked. But another few yards told a different tale. The blackened, charred building contrasted sharply against the field of pure white.

Upon close inspection, the homestead turned out to be

othing more than a bare shack. "I don't get it," Stafford aid as he walked through the empty room.

"This must be Partridge's spread," Jessie answered with udden insight.

"But Partridge never mentioned—" he began, then topped abruptly as he started to fit the pieces together.

Jessie nodded. "He burned it himself, and was going to lame it on the Indians."

"But how did he know they had left the reservation?"

"He probably didn't. But that wouldn't have mattered. After claiming the credit for shooting that Indian, everyone vould have suspected the Comanches did it for revenge. It vould have given Colonel McKenzie just cause to march gainst the Indians."

"You still think the colonel has a part in this?" Stafford sked as he knelt down and started to light a fire in the ireplace.

Jessie thought a moment. "I don't really know."

"Having no love for the Indians doesn't necessarily nake one a dishonest cheat. I should know."

"You may be right," Jessie admitted begrudgingly. "But hen how did Dineen get killed?"

"Dineen?"

"The whiskey smuggler," she answered as she moved :loser to the warmth of the fire.

"Why don't we ponder that over a hot cup of coffee? There's something else to ponder, too. How come this shack didn't burn to the ground?"

"The snow," Jessie answered quickly. "Partridge proba->ly doused the hut with kerosene. The fuel would burn apidly, but before the wood really caught the heavy snow :xtinguished the flames."

Stafford nodded. It seemed a likely explanation. He started out of the shack. "I'll get the cof—" He stopped in nidsentence as he saw the riders approaching silently hrough the deep snow. At his hesitation, Jessie also urned.

173

The lieutenant saw the feathered bonnet of the lead rider, and reached for his gun, but Jessie saw the straight, black hair and the almond-shaped eyes of the lead figure. "Ki!" she exclaimed as she went rushing to him.

Over hot coffee and beans Ki described briefly the events of the last few days. Jessie listened intently. "I figured it would be no problem to lease some cattle to the Comanches," he concluded. "Maybe even incorporate them into our organization the way we do with other small, independent ranchers."

"I don't see why not, Ki. This is pretty good grazing land," Jessie said enthusiastically. "And I'll drive them up myself to make sure the Indians get off on the right foot." She turned to Stafford. "We may even have to stay on a while to make sure they understand the ins and outs of ranching."

"I'd be willing," agreed Ki. He was remembering his last peyote vision and was looking forward to finding, and spending more time with, the beautiful squaw.

"Seems like everything is working out just peachy, 'cept for the homesteaders," Stafford said a bit sarcastically.

"There are always problems that have to be worked out between farmers and ranchers, but they're not insurmountable." Jessie was all business. "It's been done other places; it can be done here."

Stafford took her word on that. "Then all we got to do is round up that snake Tyler."

A frown formed on Jessie's face. "That may not be as easy as it seems. We don't have any solid evidence against him."

"Partridge tried to kill us!" Stafford exclaimed.

"We have no proof that Tyler had anything to do with that," Jessie explained calmly.

"We can't let him get away with this," the lieutenant said firmly.

"We won't." Jessie was just as firm.

174

"I think our friend Tyler may be guilty of more than we realize," Ki interjected into the conversation.

Jessie turned to him. "What do you mean?"

"At first it seemed like one bad situation, with lots of factors contributing to make it even worse," Ki explained calmly. "But that was before we could point to any one element as being the cause. It seems to me, as the lieutenant already stated, the heart of the whole problem stems from the homesteaders."

"We realized that before," Jessie said, unsure where Ki was leading.

"But now we also know that Tyler has been behind a lot of the trouble," continued Ki.

"From the start I wondered what Sam Caldwell's role was in this," Jessie remarked.

Stafford seemed confused. "The homesteaders and the Comanches are both fighting for their land. They both think they have a fair claim to it."

A smile crossed Ki's face. "Did you ever wonder why white homesteaders were suddenly staking out Indian land?"

Jessie didn't give Stafford time to answer. "The Comanches have a treaty signed by our government that gives them claim to this land. Now I'm awfully curious to see what the homesteaders have that entitles them to think they have a right to the very same land."

"I think we better have a talk with some of them," Stafford concluded.

Jessie agreed. "Sam Caldwell's our best bet. I trust him."

Ki had the final word. "Even more important, he trusts us."

They were still about a mile from the Caldwell place when Jessie heard the sharp crack; there was no mistaking the loud recoil of the Sharp's rifle. Jessie spurred her horse into a gallop. Stafford followed close behind. But when

they came within sight of the house everything seem
peaceful enough.

By the time Jessie, Ki, and Stafford dismounted at t'
front door—Ki's Comanche bodyguards had prudent'
chosen to make camp in the dry gully just beyond t'
house—Sam Caldwell was already there to greet ther
though this time he wasn't brandishing his carbine.

"What's all the hurry?" Sam asked his guests.

"We heard the Sharp's and thought there might be tro'
ble," Jessie explained.

"Why, thank you," Sam said with a warm smile, "b'
that was just Toby. The boy bagged him a wild turkey," l
added proudly. "Dinner'll be ready in a bit. I hope you pl'
on staying."

"That depends, Sam. We'd like to ask you a few que
tions."

"Don't see why not," he said as he ushered them in'
the warm house.

Once inside Jessie said a brief hello to Elsa and Sar'
who were busy at the stove, then got right down to bus'
ness. "Sam, did you know this was reservation land?"

"I know it used to be," he said frankly. "But now it
ours."

"What made you think you could settle here?"

"Now, Jessie, I got as much right here as the next ma'
This here's a free country. . . ."

Obviously Sam misinterpreted the question, placing th'
emphasis on the *you* instead of the *here*. Jessie tried t'
correct the misunderstanding, but Sam was so riled up h'
was barely listening.

"An' it don't matter none where someone comes fro'
or what his damned name is or anything like that," he con'
tinued without stopping. "Just so long as he's willing t'
work his claim, no one can take his land away. I got '
document from the government that says just that!"

"If you have some papers that—" Ki began, but was cu'
off by the raging homesteader.

176

"I know there are some that don't hold much stock in paper, but it's the law just the same. Those kind of folk only believe in one thing," he said as he grabbed his Winchester and gave it a menacing shake. "But we got enough of that to make 'em see the law awfully clear."

"Sam, please. We're not trying to run you off your land. We want to make sure no one else can. We'd like to see whatever documents you have," Jessie said with a reassuring calmness.

He stormed out of the room, but returned a minute later waving a piece of paper. "Here's my deed. See for yourself."

Jessie took the paper and studied it. It was an official-looking document, with a decorative gilded border. "DEPARTMENT OF THE INTERIOR" was printed boldly across the face, and the official seal of the department was stamped above the two signatures. One of which obviously belonged to Samuel Caldwell. The other, as she had half-expected, belonged to Charles Tyler. She handed the deed to Ki.

It only took him a minute to pass judgment. "It looks good, but it's a phony. Any big-city printing shop could have produced this."

"I agree." Jessie turned to the homesteader. Sam looked dumbfounded, but remained silent, his anger already spent. "Before I explain everything, Sam, I want to know one more thing. Who did you buy the land from?"

The question baffled Sam. To him the answer was plain enough. "The government!"

Jessie nodded. "But who did you actually pay the money to?"

"Charles Tyler."

Again that came as no surprise. "You'd better sit down, Sam. We have some explaining to do." She filled him in on most of the details, fitting the final pieces in as she went.

When she finished Sam looked glum. "Tyler had no right to sell any land. That means I don't really own my

177

land? It's Indian land, an' belongs to them? They can take it away from me?" With each question Sam sounded more and more incredulous.

"No, they can't," Jessie said firmly. Ki turned an interested face toward her. He was curious to hear her reasoning. Jessie addressed her answer as much to Ki as to Sam. "The Comanches are going to lease their land over to the settlers that are already here," she said flatly.

"I reckon they'll do just that," Sam said doubtfully.

"It'll be the price of the cattle. I'll lease them a herd and they'll lease their land over to the homesteaders." She turned back to Sam. "I think the Comanches can get along with the few families that are already here. They have so far."

Sam was about to object when he realized much of his so-called "Indian trouble" was really greedy white man trouble. "I hope you're right, Jessie."

"I think they'll agree to it," Ki announced.

"What makes you say that?" Sam wondered aloud.

"It's a good compromise, and I think both sides will be looking for a fair solution. Besides," he added with a touch of a smile, "I'm not without influence among the Comanches."

Their good spirits were broken by the sounds of gunfire outside the house. Sam grabbed his rifle as Toby came running in with the Sharp's. Stafford was already at the window, looking through the slat in the board. "Hold it! Those are my men." Even in the fading light Stafford could see the yellow stripes of fellow cavalrymen.

"Then what are they doing shooting at us?" Sam demanded to know.

"That's a good question."

"And there's our answer," Jessie said, pointing off to the right. They all crowded around the narrow window crack.

"It's Tyler." Stafford spoke for them all. "But what does he want? And what are those men doing with him?"

Jessie wasn't listening. She recognized one of the soldiers, and turned to Ki excitedly. "That man was guarding Dineen." It was now clear how the whiskey smuggler had been murdered. She turned back to Stafford and started to answer his question. "I have a pretty good hunch . . ." Jessie began, but stopped as Tyler shouted out his demands.

"Sam, you're harboring an army deserter and his accomplice. We're here for the lieutenant and the woman. Send them out and you won't get hurt."

"What does he want with you?" Sam asked.

"We know what he's up to," Jessie answered simply.

"But he already has our money. Why doesn't he take it and run?"

"You don't understand greedy people, Sam." Sometimes Jessie regretted the fact that she did. "That was just the beginning. He won't stop there. I think he wanted to have just enough settlers to instigate hostilities between the army and the Indians."

"But why?" Sam persisted.

"If the Indians were to get wiped out or relocate, there'd be a lot of open land. My bet is that Tyler already had first dibs on most of it. He stands to become a very wealthy man."

Outside there was another shot. "Send 'em out," Tyler repeated loudly. "I won't be asking again."

"Don't even think about it, Jessie," Sam stated flatly.

Jessie was looking past him at Elsa and her daughter, Sara. "I wouldn't want anything to happen to your family."

"I could try sneaking out after you," suggested Ki. "I don't think he knows I'm here."

Sam could see she was thinking about the possibility. "If you walk out there, do you really think he'll let us be?" His tone was skeptical. "From what you say, I wouldn't put it past him to massacre us all in the middle of the night and let the Comanches take the blame for it." Sam let out a small whistle. "That'd start the ball rolling all right. You'd have that full-scale war on your hands."

179

Jessie looked at the homesteader and knew he was right "You're learning fast," was all she said.

"Then what do we do?" Stafford asked.

"We do nothing," Sam answered. "They can't burn us out, the walls are solid 'dobe; an' they can't smoke us out, there ain't enough dry brush for that."

"But they can blow us up," Ki noted dryly from his position at the window.

One of the troopers was charging in toward the house. In his hand was an unmistakable stick of dynamite, the lighted fuse sparking brightly. A rifle sounded from within the house, and the rider toppled off his horse, holding on to his wounded shoulder.

Stafford hadn't wanted to shoot down the soldier, but he couldn't let him attack the house. He had planned to unhorse him, hoping that would stop the man's attack.

But the soldier rose to his feet, still clutching his shoulder, and continued to move toward the building, zigzagging as he ran closer. It was Toby who felled him with one shot from the powerful Sharp's. There was little chance the man was alive. After a few seconds the stick of dynamite exploded next to his body, and there was absolutely no chance.

"We can hold them off as long as we can see them, but it'll be dark inside the hour," Stafford said worriedly.

Tyler, Partridge's sidekick, Harrison, and the two remaining cavalrymen regrouped out of range. The agent must have realized the very same thing, for they seemed in no hurry to start another assault.

"Maybe I could still sneak out and outflank them," Ki suggested once more.

"Or I could try picking them off one by one," Toby said. "They might wander within range."

"One thing is certain," Stafford warned. "We can't wait till it gets dark, or it'll be too late for us."

They had no answer for that, but fortunately they needed none. With a bloodcurdling shriek, Running Wolf and his two braves descended on the unsuspecting Tyler.

The Comanches charged through the group, and continued till they were well out of gunfire range. The white men mobilized quickly, but not before one soldier lay dead, his chest pierced clear through by an arrow. And Harrison was leaning over pulling a shaft from his hip.

The Comanches turned for another assault. Tyler and his band were ready this time, but it made little difference. With the Comanches on one side and the powerful Sharp's rifle on the other, they were caught in a deadly crossfire. The last cavalryman lighted a stick of dynamite, but before he could throw it into the Indian's midst he fell off his horse backward, his body stuck with numerous arrows.

After a very quick assessment Tyler mounted a horse and took flight, with Harrison right in his dust. Whooping joyously, the two braves took up the chase. The white men would never be seen alive again.

Meanwhile, Running Wolf raced up to the house and called our loudly, "Spirit HalfBreed." He seemed greatly relieved when Ki stepped out, obviously unharmed.

Sam heard the approaching horses, but waited for the knock at the door before getting up from the table. He opened the door, and a man's voice filled the room. "Excuse me, sir, we're looking for some army deserters, and renegade Comanches. . . ."

At the sound of the voice Stafford sprung up from his chair.

"Come on in, Colonel," Sam said warmly.

Colonel McKenzie entered the house and stopped short at what he saw. "Stafford! What are you doing here?"

The lieutenant saluted crisply. "I'm here to report that, ah, I've found the deserters, sir, but they were killed while resisting arrest."

"Oh?" the colonel said with a raised eyebrow. He turned his attention to the three Indians who sat at the Caldwells' dinner table. Stafford continued to stammer. "Ah, and the renegade Indians are returning to their village. They should be back in a few days. Running Wolf, Dark Cloud, and Round Stone were coming in with me as a sign of good faith."

"Oh, really, Lieutenant?" McKenzie eyed the group suspiciously.

"Yes, sir."

"I'll expect a full report on my desk." The colonel turned crisply on his heels. "Carry on," he commanded, then was out the door.

They all broke out laughing. Jessie looked around the table. Here, sitting down to a turkey dinner, were representatives of all the opposing factions: white man and red man, farmer and rancher, soldier and brave, even foreigner and native. And for the first time both the Comanches and the Caldwells looked at ease and relaxed. Or at least, the Indians looked as relaxed as they could be sitting in their straight-backed chairs, struggling with their knives and forks. It was just a beginning, but it spoke well of the future.

Ki was thinking similar thoughts, but he felt a vague sense of loss. He picked up his feathered bonnet, which he had laid aside when they sat down to eat, and stroked the smooth eagle feathers. He stared at the Comanches and seemed to be weighing something in his mind. Slowly a smile crossed his face as he turned and looked at the youngest Caldwell.

Jessie followed Ki's stare. James's eight-year-old eyes had not moved from the Comanches, but there was no fear in them, only youthful wonder. Jessie recalled her childhood fears and tried to imagine what her reaction to dinner with a bunch of Comanches would have been. She smiled at the thought. *Yes, it's just a start,* she told herself, *but a very good one at that.*

Watch for

LONE STAR AND THE NEVADA MUSTANGS

fifty-first novel in the exciting
LONE STAR
series from Jove

coming in November!

☆ **From the Creators of LONGARM** ☆

The Wild West will never be the same!

LONE STAR

LONE STAR features the extraordinary and
beautiful Jessica Starbuck and her loyal half-
American half-Japanese martial arts sidekick, Ki.

_ LONE STAR AND THE BIGGEST GUN IN THE WEST #36	08332-1/$2.50
_ LONE STAR AND THE APACHE WARRIOR #37	08344-5/$2.50
_ LONE STAR AND THE GOLD MINE WAR #38	08368-2/$2.50
_ LONE STAR AND THE ALASKAN GUNS #40	08423-9/$2.50
_ LONE STAR AND THE WHITE RIVER CURSE #41	08446-8/$2.50
_ LONE STAR AND THE TOMBSTONE GAMBLE #42	08462-X/$2.50
_ LONE STAR AND THE TIMBERLAND TERROR #43	08496-4/$2.50
_ LONE STAR IN THE CHEROKEE STRIP #44	08515-4/$2.50
_ LONE STAR AND THE OREGON RAIL SABOTAGE #45	08570-7/$2.50
_ LONE STAR AND THE MISSION WAR #46	08581-2/$2.50
_ LONE STAR AND THE GUNPOWDER CORE #47	08608-8/$2.50
_ LONE STAR AND THE LAND BARONS #48	08649-5/$2.50
_ LONE STAR AND THE GOLF PIRATES #49	08676-2/$2.75

Available at your local bookstore or return this form to:

 JOVE
THE BERKLEY PUBLISHING GROUP, Dept. B
390 Murray Hill Parkway, East Rutherford, NJ 07073

Please send me the titles checked above. I enclose _____. Include $1.00 for postage
and handling if one book is ordered; add 25¢ per book for two or more not to exceed
$1.75. CA, IL, NJ, NY, PA, and TN residents please add sales tax. Prices subject to change
without notice and may be higher in Canada. Do not send cash.

NAME_____

ADDRESS_____

CITY_____STATE/ZIP_____

(Allow six weeks for delivery.)

54

LONGARM

Explore the exciting Old West with one of the men who made it wild!

___08374-7	LONGARM AND THE PAINTED DESERT #69	$2.50
___06271-5	LONGARM ON THE OGALLALA TRAIL #70	$2.50
___07915-4	LONGARM ON THE ARKANSAS DIVIDE #71	$2.50
___06273-1	LONGARM AND THE BLIND MAN'S VENGEANCE #72	$2.50
___08173-6	LONGARM ON THE NEVADA LINE #76	$2.50
___08190-6	LONGARM AND THE BLACKFOOT GUNS #77	$2.50
___08232-5	LONGARM AND THE COWBOY'S REVENGE #79	$2.50
___08331-3	LONGARM ON THE GOODNIGHT TRAIL #80	$2.50
___08343-7	LONGARM AND THE FRONTIER DUTCHESS #81	$2.50
___08367-4	LONGARM IN THE BITTERROOTS #82	$2.50
___08396-8	LONGARM AND THE TENDERFOOT #83	$2.50
___08422-0	LONGARM AND THE STAGECOACH BANDITS #84	$2.50
___08445-X	LONGARM AND THE BIG SHOOT-OUT #85	$2.50
___08461-1	LONGARM IN THE HARD ROCK COUNTRY #86	$2.50
___08495-6	LONGARM IN THE TEXAS PANHANDLE #87	$2.50
___08514-6	LONGARM AND THE RANCHER'S SHOWDOWN #88	$2.50
___08569-3	LONGARM AND THE INLAND PASSAGE #89	$2.50
___08580-4	LONGARM IN THE RUBY RANGE COUNTRY #90	$2.50
___08607-X	LONGARM AND THE GREAT CATTLE KILL #91	$2.50
___08648-7	LONGARM AND THE CROOKED RAILMAN #92	$2.50
___08675-4	LONGARM ON THE SIWASH TRAIL #93	$2.75
___08715-7	LONGARM AND THE RUNAWAY THIEVES #94	$2.75

Prices may be slightly higher in Canada.

Available at your local bookstore or return this form to:

JOVE
THE BERKLEY PUBLISHING GROUP, Dept. B
390 Murray Hill Parkway, East Rutherford, NJ 07073

Please send me the titles checked above. I enclose _____. Include $1.00 for postage and handling if one book is ordered; add 25¢ per book for two or more not to exceed $1.75. CA, IL, NJ, NY, PA, and TN residents please add sales tax. Prices subject to change without notice and may be higher in Canada. Do not send cash.

NAME_____

ADDRESS_____

CITY_____ STATE/ZIP_____

(Allow six weeks for delivery.)